"...Your Way ... with Me."

Jason laughed lightly at Zandra's teasing, but his eyes sparkled with desire. He rose from the table, gently guiding her into the bedchamber.

He was slipping the rose peignoir from her shoulders, pressing her against him, his hands playing over her throat, her shoulders, her back. "So lovely, so lovely," he said huskily, and he kissed her lips, softly at first, then with mounting ardor.

Zandra was aware of nothing but his lean, hard body pressed against her as rigid as iron. Her hands moved over his body, caressing the hard muscles of his arms and back, stroking the coarse hair of his chest, moving down the narrow hips. There was not an inch of his body that she did not yearn for. In that moment, she knew she wanted him as desperately, as achingly as he wanted her.

Before Jason blew out the three candles beside the bed, Zandra remembered the words of the marriage ceremony. "With my body I thee worship." She understood now their full meaning.

Dear Reader,

We, the editors of Tapestry Romances, are committed to bringing you two outstanding original romantic historical novels each and every month.

From Kentucky in the 1850s to the court of Louis XIII, from the deck of a pirate ship within sight of Gibraltar to a mining camp high in the Sierra Nevadas, our heroines experience life and love, romance and adventure.

Our aim is to give you the kind of historical romances that you want to read. We would enjoy hearing your thoughts about this book and all future Tapestry Romances. Please write to us at the address below.

The Editors
Tapestry Romances
POCKET BOOKS
1230 Avenue of the Americas
Box TAP
New York, N.Y. 10020

Ardent Vows

Helen Tucker

A TAPESTRY BOOK
PUBLISHED BY POCKET BOOKS NEW YORK

An *Original* publication of TAPESTRY BOOKS

 A Tapestry Book published by
POCKET BOOKS, a division of Simon & Schuster, Inc.
1230 Avenue of the Americas, New York, N.Y. 10020

ISBN: 0-671-49780-4

First Tapestry Books printing December, 1983

10 9 8 7 6 5 4 3 2 1

Ardent Vows

Prologue

SHE WOULD NOT BE DRAGGED KICKING AND screaming to the altar but only because she knew it would do nothing to prevent the wedding. If she had thought it would even postpone the ceremony, she would at this moment be screaming loud enough to be heard three counties distant. Instead, she was standing quietly beside her father just outside the heavy oak doors of St. John's-in-the-Woods waiting to hear the swelling tones of the organ.

Only the somber expression on Alexandra Coulter's usually smiling and animated face marred the perfect appearance she made as she waited for what was supposed to be the happiest moment of a girl's life. Her gown of the most delicate white lace over an underskirt of white satin had come from London's famous modiste, Madame Celine. The high-necked satin bodice and long sleeves were embroidered with tiny seed pearls, a few of which also adorned the end of the fingertip veil. (The one blessing of the day, she thought, was that her face would be hidden behind the white cloud of the veil. People could only guess at her misery without knowing for sure.) The gown's train was so long that when she reached the altar, it would extend more than halfway down the aisle of the small church. It would be like the anchor of a ship, holding her in place.

Her dark auburn hair was pulled into a bun at the nape of her neck, making her appear older than her eighteen years; the intense, solemn expression in her vividly green eyes also belied her actual age. Her mouth was pressed into a thin line as though it would never extend into a smile again. It also looked as if she were trying with all her might to keep from saying something scathing to the man on whose arm she was leaning.

Which was exactly what she was doing.

She felt betrayed by her father, who, until a few weeks ago, could do no wrong in her eyes. At this moment she hated him so intensely that she could not even think of words that would express it. Lemuel Coulter was forcing her, literally *forcing her,* into marriage with a man she scarcely knew and certainly did not love. She had begged, implored, cajoled and beseeched; she had cried, raged, howled and screeched, to no avail.

"You are thinking only of yourself," she had said to him just last night. "You are selfish and mean. You only want to get rid of me so you can marry your trollop."

She had never before spoken to her father in that manner. Lemuel, who had been sitting across from his widowed sister, Emerald Wallace, in the library, rose angrily. "You will never speak of Mrs. Mayhew with disrespect again," he said between clenched teeth. "The idea! Calling that admirable lady a . . . what you called her."

"She is . . ." Alexandra began, only to be silenced by Lemuel's thundering cry of "Silence!"

For about thirty seconds the only sound to be heard in the room was the exaggeratedly loud ticking of the little ormolu clock on the mantel above the fireplace.

"Well, she is," Alexandra said finally, determined to have the last word about the woman her father was about to bring into the house as mistress. "And you are."

"I am what?" Lemuel asked, obviously struggling to remain calm.

"What I said—selfish and mean."

"It strikes me, my girl, that you are being exactly those things of which you are accusing me."

Alexandra crossed the room and stood beside his chair. "I am nothing of the kind. I would *never* ask a daughter of mine to leave my house. And I would *never* throw my sister out."

At this, Emerald's eyebrows went up about a half inch, but she continued to hold her peace, looking down at the embroidery in her lap. She was four years younger than her brother's fifty-two and looked nothing like him. When they stood side by side, his rotundity was emphasized by her reediness, and where his dark hair had given way to gray, hers had kept its color. She was usually placid and serene, he almost always on the verge of, or deep into, one emotion or another: joy, rage, inquisitiveness, satisfaction.

Now Lemuel stood up beside his daughter and trembled with anger. "As you very well know, I am not throwing my sister out, Alexandra. She has elected to make her home with you and your husband, thinking she might be of some help to you in your new life."

"My new life!" She spat the words out. "I was very happy with my old life. At least, I could have been had you not decided to ruin it . . . and had you been a man of your word. You said I could go to London for a season. You promised me!"

Emerald looked up. She spoke for the first time. "You did promise her that, Lem."

4

"Stay out of this, Emma," her brother barked. "I promised Kate on her deathbed that I would always do what was best for Alexandra, that I would be both mother and father to her. *That* promise supersedes all others. Besides," he returned his attention to Alexandra, "you would find no gaiety in London now, no reason to want to be there. Prince George has not been dead a year and Queen Anne's court will remain in mourning for a long time to come. There are also rumors that the Queen's health is so wretched that she may never entertain again."

"There are even rumors from time to time that she has died," Emerald put in. "If I have heard it once, I have heard it a dozen times: 'Queen Anne is dead.' It has become a cliché."

"Please believe me, Alexandra," Lemuel said, an almost pleading tone in his voice. "I am doing what I think is best for you."

"You call forcing me to marry a man I don't love doing what is best for me?"

"Stop sounding like a naive child!" Lemuel said. "You are a mature, intelligent woman, so please try to act like one. What has love to do with anything?"

"Everything!" She sat down in the chair beside Emerald. "Are you implying that there is no love involved in your match with Mrs. Mayhew?" She still could not believe that her father, after all these years, was going to be married again, and to a woman such as Mrs. Mayhew after beautiful, gracious Kate.

"Ah-hem!" Lemuel cleared his throat. "We have the deepest respect for each other—which I hope you and your husband will have once you are married and get to know each other."

"There!" she cried triumphantly. "Did you hear him, Aunt? In that one sentence he has stated what is wrong with this whole business —and God knows it's more of a business than a marriage. Jason Braley and I should get to know each other *before* we are married, not after. We could find that we despised each other beyond endurance—which I think we probably do."

"Child, child, you must get rid of your romantic notions about love and marriage," Lemuel told her. "They will be the ruin of you."

"First you say I am mature, then you call me a child," Alexandra said. "Frankly, Father, I don't think you know your own mind. For that matter, I am no longer sure you even have one."

"Alexandra!" Emerald said, raising her voice one decibel above a whisper. "Mature woman or child, you should show more respect. Lem really is trying to do what he thinks is best for you."

Ignoring her, Alexandra continued, "What

would you say if I flatly refused to go through with the marriage?"

"I would say that we already have discussed that prospect no less than twenty times in the past month and I have no intention of listening to your nonsense on that subject again." With that Lemuel stomped out of the room. They heard the front door slam as he went outside for a walk.

Tomorrow she was to be married, and she still couldn't figure out how it had happened so fast. First, there had been her father's sudden attachment to that woman. Kate, Alexandra's mother, had died nine years before. A few months later, Emerald, a recent widow, moved into her brother's house near Beaconsfield. The woman and the ten-year-old girl, having grief in common, got along well from the beginning, and Alexandra came to think of Emerald as a friend.

After Kate's death, Lemuel became something of a recluse, his one concession to conviviality being the Christmas Eve supper to which he invited the families from neighboring estates and nearby Beaconsfield. Alexandra could not be sure, but she thought she might have seen Jason Braley for the first time at one of those suppers. Other than that, there were only two times when she clearly remembered seeing him before.

On the first occasion, she had turned her

gig into the drive leading to the large, rambling house when she saw him approaching. He stopped his team as she came alongside, calling, "Good afternoon, Miss Coulter."

She stopped also, staring at him. He had dark brown hair that curled just over his high collar, brown eyes that seemed to be laughing at something. Those eyes also seemed to be looking right through her, as though they could see right through to bone and fiber, muscle and blood. After they had raked her body, causing a shiver to go through her, they fastened on her face as though no thought of hers could possibly remain secret from such probing.

He seemed to be in his middle twenties. He was very tall—she could tell that even though he was sitting—and muscular. He would have been handsome, *very* handsome, she thought, except that a slight gauntness of face gave him a somewhat shrewd, calculating look.

"I don't believe I know you, sir," she said, though he did look familiar.

He gave her a slow, lazy smile. "We have met." He paused for a moment. "I am Jason Braley. I live down the road," he pointed, "about ten miles."

She remembered having heard her father speak of the Braleys occasionally over the years, but since the two families never exchanged calls, she connected no faces with the name. About a year ago, she recalled,

8

Angus Braley had died and Lemuel had re-marked, "I guess young Jason will be Squire Braley now. He will have his hands too full with the farm to go racketing around the county anymore."

"Yes, I believe I have heard my father speak of you," she told him now, ready to continue up the drive.

He looked as though he wanted to detain her but wasn't sure how to. Then, as she flicked the ribbons over her horse's back, he unac-countably reached out and caught hold of the reins, deterring her progress.

"I'd like to speak to you, if I may," he said.

"About what?" she asked, mystified.

"About . . ." he began, then hesitated. "I say, could we go back toward the house—maybe to the garden for a bit?"

"A bit of what?" She looked at him specula-tively.

"A bit of a chat, Miss Coulter." He returned her stare, appraising her as though she were a new blood about to go to the auction block.

"I think not," she told him. He must have had business with her father, otherwise he would not be coming from Coulter Manor, but even so, for him to try to strike up an ac-quaintance with her in the drive was an odd way of doing things. It showed rather abomi-nable manners on his part, she thought. Yet there was something about him—she could not have said what—that strongly attracted

9

her, causing her to be slightly irritated with herself and more than slightly irritated with him.

"Why not?" he persisted. "I do believe you could spare me a few moments of your time if you wanted to."

"You have gone right to the heart of the matter, Mr. Braley," she declared. "I do not want to. I can think of nothing whatever that we have to converse about." Those eyes. She wished he would not stare at her so.

"I can think of several things," he told her, a devilish grin spreading across his face. "Starting with . . ."

"Good day to you, Mr. Braley." She snatched the ribbons, which he still held loosely in his left hand, set her horse into a trot and, without looking back, left him at the foot of the drive. She could hear him laughing and her irritation turned to fury. She had heard enough about his reputation to make her wary of his advances. Her father might make an unsuitable match for himself, but it was hardly likely that he would ever let her associate with a rogue like Jason Braley.

She wondered why he seemed to recognize her at once, while she had had no idea who he was until he introduced himself. It was possible that when she was younger and hadn't noticed "older men," she and Braley had been at social affairs together. She knew that he had been away at school and later at university for some years. It was too bad that during all that schooling he had not learned better manners. He seemed determined to live up to his reputation.

Later that afternoon when she joined Emerald for tea, she was surprised to find her father and Mrs. Mayhew there also. Mrs. Mayhew was overdressed for the occasion, her portly body stuffed into a violet silk gown with ruffles from waist to hem. Her hair, curled to a fine friz, was an unusual shade of red—henna straight from the bottle, Alexandra and Emerald had agreed.

Under the circumstances, Alexandra could not question her father about his visit from Braley that afternoon nor tell him about her strange encounter. By the next morning, she'd forgotten it. Mrs. Mayhew had driven everything else out of her mind. It was becoming increasingly obvious to Alexandra and Emerald that something was afoot. "It isn't what you're thinking," Emerald told Alexandra, "or she would never come here, at least not until after some kind of declaration from Lem." But it was soon apparent that it was exactly what Alexandra was thinking, and so she forgot about Jason Braley . . . until two weeks later.

She and Emerald were in the morning room when Elton, the butler, told her Mr. Coulter would like to see her in the library.

She thought she detected a sudden pallor in

Emerald's cheeks, but all Emerald said was, "You had better see what Lem wants."

She started into the room, then stopped at the door when she saw her father talking with Jason Braley.

"Come in, my dear," Lemuel said, noticing her. "I believe you know our visitor."

Alexandra nodded to Braley but did not speak. It was almost as though she were seeing him for the first time, and that strange attraction he had for her was registering anew in her mind. His eyes still looked at her as though they knew all her secrets but would never reveal their own. He was even taller than she had thought, well over six feet, and he was better looking also, though not what she would call a really handsome man. There was too much of a rugged, outdoor look about him for him to pass as handsome, but as far as his dress went, he was in the first stare of fashion. He wore dove gray breeches with white stockings, a darker coat of Bath super-fine and a neckcloth so intricately tied as to leave the viewer awestruck.

In the first stare of fashion, yes—but at ten-thirty in the morning? Why was he at Coulter Manor dressed like that at this hour?

"How do you do, Miss Coulter?" Braley moved closer to her, smiling broadly. "Since you seemed apprehensive about talking with me alone recently, I thought the best way to assure myself of your attention was to have Mr. Coulter present."

"I still can think of nothing whatever that we have to discuss, Mr. Braley." She did not know whether she was more angry with him for causing her heart to beat so rapidly or with herself for letting him affect her so.

"Sit down, Alexandra," Lemuel said when it seemed apparent that Braley was not going to answer.

She went to a chair, but before she was seated her father continued. "Squire Braley has come to ask for your hand in marriage, and I have given my consent."

Her legs suddenly gave way and she sat down with a plop. For at least two minutes she was speechless; then she exclaimed, "Father, your wits have gone begging!"

"Now, now," he tried to silence her before she said something that might end the betrothal before it actually began. "I think when you and Jason have some time together, you will see . . . I will just step outside for a while and . . ." Embarrassed as well as momentarily muddled by his daughter's unexpected rudeness to young Braley, as well as her impertinence to her own father, Lemuel started to leave the room, but Alexandra was out of her chair as suddenly as if she had just discovered a fire beneath it.

"No, *I* will go out and let the two of you get better acquainted," she said. "I have no reason to want to know Mr. Braley better, but apparently you do, Father."

Much to her consternation, Jason Braley obviously found this amusing, for he laughed heartily.

"I am glad I afford you so much amusement, Mr. Braley," she said indignantly.

"I am beginning to get the idea that life with you could be very entertaining, Miss Coulter," he answered.

"I am afraid you will have to find your entertainment elsewhere," she said, "as I understand you are accustomed to do." With that, she swept past him and out of the room. She left the house and went to the garden, trying desperately to make some sense out of this completely nonsensical happening.

About a half hour later, her father found her there. "Our visitor has gone," he said.

"*Your* visitor," she said. "He was not here at my invitation."

"You have never been impertinent before, Alexandra," he said mildly. "It does not become you. The lad came here because he wants to marry you. And I have agreed. The wedding will take place next month."

Paling to the color of the stone bench, she could only stare at him, mouth agape.

"It will be for the best," he went on, his tone of voice as soothing as balm. "You see, my dear, the Widow Mayhew and I are planning matrimony and she—that is, we think we can get a better start as man and wife without young ones around to . . ."

"Dear God!" she breathed. "You sound as though I were eight years old instead of eighteen. Anyway, you do not have to marry me off to get rid of me. You promised to give me a season in London this year, so Emma and I will go to London and leave you and your precious Mayhem all to yourselves."

"Mayhew," he corrected automatically. "I am sorry, Alexandra, but it is out of the question now. I think my way is better. Look at it this way: why do young ladies have a season in London? To attract a wellborn, eligible man for a husband, of course. You have managed to do that without the trouble and expense of going to London."

"But I don't want to marry Jason Braley!" She was almost shouting now.

Lemuel stood up. "I see there is no point in talking to you at this time. Perhaps when you are calmer and can see things in a more rational way . . ." He left her, striding purposefully back to the house, already deep in plans for the wedding.

Nothing Alexandra could do or say could dissuade him from that end. She did, however, confound him by refusing to see Braley again before the wedding, thinking that that would give her father second thoughts on the matter. But it only turned out to be a case of stubborner meeting stubbornest.

As she stood in her bedchamber on the eve of her wedding looking disconsolately at her trunk, it occurred to her—and not for the first time—that she could run away from Coulter Manor. But—also not for the first time—she discarded the idea as totally impractical. Where would she go and what would she do with no money? Though she was extremely well read, her education at the Beaconsfield Academy for Young Females had been only rudimentary: music, sewing, painting and French. It certainly would not qualify her as a governess. How else could she earn a living? As a maid or servant? As a shop-girl?

There was no help for it; within the next twelve hours she would become Jason Braley's wife.

She went to the window and looked out into the dark night. There was no moon and not a star was visible. The night perfectly matched her mood: black on black. For years she had dreamed of marriage to a man she loved and respected, a man who would be her friend as well as her husband, someone with whom she could discuss books and drama and music, even politics, though she knew that women were supposed to have no knowledge of or interest in that subject. She had dreamed of living in London where she would meet the people who would make those dreams come true.

If she were absolutely truthful, she would have to admit that there was something about Jason Braley that appealed to her, caused her pulse to race and her breath to catch when she was in his presence. But there also was something about him that infuriated her, probably his self-assurance, his arrogance. And as for marriage to him . . . For the tiniest second she wondered what it would be like to have him make love to her and an inner excitement such as she had never experienced before all but overcame her.

But it was folly to think like that, she told herself sharply. After all, marriage to him would involve little love and much boredom. She had lived her entire life in the country and now, as she matured, she wanted, she needed, something else.

A little while later, when she heard the front door open and her father enter the house, she decided impulsively to try to reason with him.

By the time she reached the foot of the stairs, she could hear him talking to Emerald in the sitting room.

"Can't you do something with her, Emma?" Lemuel asked. "I thought if another woman talked to her it might—"

"The only talk that will do any good is if you tell her the truth, Lem," Emerald interrupted. "I think you might find her more understanding if she knew the circumstances."

"Never!" Lemuel exclaimed. "And I do not want to hear any more on that subject, Emma. Not another word. Now, for God's sake, let's talk about something else. I have long since been satiated with the subject of tomorrow's wedding."

Alexandra crept back upstairs, knowing there was no use in wasting more words on her father now.

Much later, there was a light tap at her door, and before she could answer, Emerald entered.

Alexandra was already in bed, holding a book in her hand, though she had not read a page and had no idea what the book was. She laid it aside and motioned for Emerald to sit on the foot of the bed.

"There is something that I must know at once," Alexandra told her. "What is this 'truth' that Father refuses to tell me?"

Startled by the question, Emerald looked at Alexandra for several seconds, then said, "Obviously you have been listening through doors, and you are old enough to know that you will never hear what you want to hear that way."

"Then perhaps you will be good enough to tell me what I want to hear?" Alexandra said, ready to vent her anger on Emerald now.

"I think what you want to hear is how to get out of being the wife of Jason Braley. Am I correct?"

"Absolutely!"

"There is no way to get out of the wedding," Emerald said, "but there is a way to get out of being his wife. Lemuel has done what he thinks is best—and in all truth, I might have done the same were I in his place—but I also can see your side of it, and I do not think you should be sentenced to spend the rest of your life on the Braley farm if that is not what you want."

"At long last somebody makes sense around here." Alexandra raised her eyes upward in thanksgiving. "But if the wedding cannot be stopped, how can I get out of living with him once we are married?"

"An annulment," Emerald said. "That is what you want: to have the marriage annulled immediately. There are two ways to go about it. First of all, if you have reservations in your mind when you take your vows, if you make promises you have no intention of keeping, that is valid reason for an annulment. And secondly . . ." She leaned forward and whispered in Alexandra's ear, her face reddening with a blush as she talked.

When she stopped, Alexandra looked at her for a moment in silence. Then she said, "You always were one for using euphemisms, Emerald. What you are really saying is that if I refuse to let Jason Braley make love to me, the marriage can be annulled."

"That is what I said." Emerald picked at the coverlet in her embarrassment.

Alexandra laughed out loud for the first time in weeks. "No, dear Aunt, what you said was that if I refused to do my wifely duty the marriage would not be considered valid. Wifely duty could include anything from managing the household staff to entertaining the guests." She was laughing again, both in merriment and in relief at having found a solution to her problem. But then she put her arms around the woman who had been friend, mother and aunt to her for the past eight years. "I do thank you for that information. It would never have entered my head. All I could think about was running away, but now . . ." She was laughing again, this time just because it felt so good to do so.

Tomorrow the wedding would take place as planned. By afternoon she would be Mrs. Jason Braley. But on the day after tomorrow she would make it as clear as her wedding crystal that she had no intention whatever of keeping a name that she had not chosen. How long did it take to get an annulment? she wondered.

Lemuel was patting the satin-clad arm tucked through his. "It is time, Alexandra. Please smile."

She was brought back to the here and now. She looked up at her father and gave him the closest thing to a smile he had seen from her for a month. He probably thought she was reconciled to this miserable marriage.

She could see down the aisle to where the vicar awaited the bride. At the altar was her bridegroom, but she could see only his profile. The little church was full. It looked as if the whole countryside had come to the wedding.

The music from the small pipe organ fairly shook the rafters as she and Lemuel began to walk down the aisle. She knew she trembled slightly but there was no help for it. Was it her imagination or was her father actually shaking a bit himself? Why should he? she thought bitterly. It was she who was being led like a lamb to the slaughter.

She looked toward her groom. He was facing her now, and involuntarily she caught her breath. He really looked quite handsome in his matching midnight blue coat and breeches with the white neckcloth over the ruffled blouse. His dark brown eyes looked almost like velvet as they focused on her with an intense, hypnotizing look. What was he thinking? she wondered. She imagined no one had ever been able to tell from his eyes.

Then she and her father were standing in

front of the vicar. The organ was hardly audible as the vicar's voice, deep and resonant, began the ceremony of the Solemnization of Matrimony.

"Dearly beloved, we are gathered together here in the sight of God and in the face of this congregation to join together this man and this woman in holy matrimony . . ."

Alexandra was not listening. She was thinking of Emerald's words last night. *First of all, if you have reservations in your mind when you take your vows, if you make promises you do not intend to keep, that is valid reason for annulment.* The promises she was about to make were to be made under duress, therefore no one, God included, could hold her to them.

"I require and charge you both, as you will answer at the dreadful day of judgment when the secrets of all hearts shall be disclosed, that if either of you know any impediment, why you may not be lawfully joined together in matrimony, you do now confess it. For be you well assured, that so many as are coupled together otherwise than God's Word does allow are not joined together by God; neither is their matrimony lawful."

She began to tremble again. Emerald had been right; an annulment would not be difficult, but listening to the words read from the Prayer Book was frightening.

Then came the first of the vows for Jason:

he promised to love her, comfort her, honor her and keep her in sickness and in health and forsaking all others, to keep only unto her so long as they both lived. His "I will" seemed to sound and then echo through the church, but when she was asked next to repeat the vows, her "I will" was so low that the vicar looked at her for a second or two as though unsure she had answered at all.

"Who giveth this woman to be married to this man?"

Lemuel placed her hand upon Jason's, stepped back, and then he took his seat beside Emerald in the front row.

Alexandra was aware that Jason was looking down at her, but she did not look up to see his expression.

At that moment, it occurred to her for the first time to wonder why he wanted to marry her. Surely there was a plenitude of young ladies about the countryside who would have fainted with joy at the prospect of becoming his bride. Why, then, had he singled out the most reluctant of all on whom to bestow his name? Were her earlier suspicions correct, that her father had wanted her out of the house so much that he would even go to such unheard-of lengths as to *ask* Braley to take her off his hands?

The thought caused her ire to grow to such intensity that when she next had to speak her vows, there was an unmistakable note of anger in her voice as she took Jason as her wedded husband.

Unless he is planning murder tonight, she thought, we will part much sooner than death.

Then he took her left hand in his and was placing a ring upon her finger, a circle of gold with at least a dozen small diamonds in it, saying, "With this ring, I thee wed, and with my body, I thee worship, and with all my worldly goods, I thee endow."

For an instant, she was acutely aware of his lean, strong body beside her, and she wondered for the second time what it would be like to have him worship her with his body. She had not known that phrase was in the marriage ceremony. Her breath grew short and she felt the blood pulsing through her. Perhaps if she and Jason had met and married under different circumstances . . . But there was no point in thinking about that now.

She returned her attention to the ceremony just as the vicar pronounced that they were man and wife together.

Jason turned her toward him and pushed back her veil. For a moment she thought he was going to kiss her, but instead, he put her hand in the crook of his arm and they walked down the aisle together and out of the church.

It was all over now, except the part she dreaded most. She had stood by Jason in the reception line, accepting the best wishes of some two hundred people. Then she had sat beside him at the sumptuous wedding breakfast, scarcely noticing the delicacies on her plate. Once in a while her eyes went down the table to her father, seated beside Mrs. Mayhew, and when her fury started to mount she would look toward Emerald, seated on the other side of the room. Only the thought that Emerald was to come to the Braley house by ten the next morning to pick her up had a calming effect. This morning Emerald had rented rooms for herself and Alexandra at the Beaconsfield Inn. This arrangement would have to suffice until more permanent quarters could be found in London.

As soon as the last toast was made, Jason whisked her into his carriage and they started for the Braley house.

"Since you have never even seen where you are to live the rest of your life, I think we might honeymoon there," he had told her during the breakfast. "Later we can take a trip to any place that especially appeals to you."

Imagine not having discussed any of this with one's betrothed before the wedding, she thought. They actually had discussed nothing whatever, she realized. Her fault, she knew—but did it really matter when by this time tomorrow they would be separated forever?

Braley Acres was not at all what she expected. The house, built of gray stone and set in a thicket of beeches, was much larger than she had thought it would be—larger even than Coulter Manor. A reception hall was just inside the entryway, and eight servants, five women and three men, were lined up to meet their new mistress. Jason presented them to her, the maids curtsying, the men bowing, and it was apparent to her that, because they thought a great deal of Jason, they were prepared to like her too.

Jason then took her on a tour of the house and she looked around curiously at everything. The house was decorated in good taste, but it badly needed redoing, she thought. It had been too long without a woman's touch to soften a bit here, lighten a bit there.

But that was, after all, no concern of hers.

The last room into which he took her was the master bedroom. It was a large corner room with windows on two sides. The first thing she saw in the room was the huge four-poster bed. The velvet draperies at the windows were of dark blue and the Persian rug on the floor was of the same color.

"This is the prettiest room in the house," she said, but then she regretted saying it for fear that he might mistake her meaning.

He smiled at her and seemed to relax. "I am glad you think so. I have just had it done over. I decided not to do the rest of the house, but to wait and let you do things the way you want them."

She nodded and looked away, afraid to meet his eyes.

"You look a bit worn—and no wonder," he said. "I suppose I should have waited until tomorrow to show you the house, but I wanted you to learn your way around and feel at home as soon as possible."

"I *am* tired." She took it up immediately, thinking that he had given her the perfect opening. She could plead fatigue, go to bed and pretend to be asleep until tomorrow morning when Emerald came for her.

"Then instead of going to the dining parlor, we shall have a light supper right here." He went to the bell cord beside the fireplace, then changed his mind. "I will go down and tell them in the kitchen, and you can change from your finery into . . . whatever is more comfortable."

He left the room before she could answer. She went to the mirror stand beside the wardrobe and looked at herself. Her pale rose traveling suit and matching hat decorated with a jaunty ostrich plume seemed ludicrous in view of the fact that she had only traveled ten miles. She took off the hat and unpinned her hair, letting the auburn tresses fall about her shoulders. She ignored the white silk gown and peignoir that Emerald had insisted must go into her trousseau, and chose a modest long-sleeved, high-necked, dark green nightgown with matching wrapper. The color made her green eyes seem even darker.

When Jason returned, she was seated in a rocking chair beside one of the windows, brushing her hair.

Before she knew what he was about, he crossed the room in four strides, put his hands on her shoulders and bent down and kissed her on the lips, at first tentatively, and then firmly, with increasing pressure. "I am going to have to get you a vanity where you can sit to brush your hair," he murmured. "That is one thing I forgot." Then he was kissing her again, his hands moving down her arms to her waist, which they encircled.

At first she was rigid under his mouth, his hands, and then, to her amazement, she found the kiss beginning to stir her. She was hardly aware that when he knelt beside her chair and pulled her to him, her body was already straining toward him. This time his kiss was deep and probing and hungry. Involuntarily, her arms went around his neck and she found herself responding as though she were as ravenously love-hungry as he. Then, suddenly remembering herself, she pulled away from him so fast that he could only look at her in bewilderment.

Apparently thinking her reluctance was due to the delicacy and shyness of his bride, he kissed her gently on the forehead and stood up. "Martin, the butler, will bring us a light supper in about ten minutes," he said.

When the food arrived, Alexandra felt half starved. Looking out one of the windows at the fading light as Martin prepared a table in the center of the room, she suddenly felt she could eat anything set before her.

The "light" supper consisted of partridge and dried salmon, broiled mushrooms, vegetables in cream sauce, fluffy rolls dripping with freshly churned butter and a plate of French pastry. There was also a basket of fruit and a platter of cheeses. There was no pretense at conversation while she and Jason did justice to Cook's work.

After they had finished, Jason looked at her uncertainly for a moment, then went to a love seat beside one of the wide windows. "Come sit over here with me," he invited.

Her better judgment told her not to comply, but she could think of no adequate reason for denying his request. She walked slowly to the love seat and sat down.

He sat down beside her, taking her left hand in his right. For a second he stroked the wedding band on her finger. "I think it is time for us to get better acquainted. Past time, but you seemed to have some difficulty in making up your mind that you wanted to know me at all."

"I had not the slightest difficulty," she said quickly. "My mind was made up from the moment my father first told me that you had offered for me. I had no inclination whatsoever to get married. That is nothing against you, understand," she added hastily.

He nodded. "I think I understand. But would it not have been easier on both of us if you had allowed me to conduct a normal courtship? As it is . . ." he broke off, looking at her.

"Why should we have had a normal courtship when there was nothing else normal about the situation?"

Jason grinned, an impish look on his face. "I can think of several things that at least approached normal, but I will not upset your sensibilities by mentioning them. Suffice it to say that I was smitten by you years ago."

"You were?" She looked at him unbelievingly. "When did we meet? I do not remember seeing you before that day in the lane when you tried to talk to me."

"I don't think we were formally introduced," he said. "I saw you at one of the Christmas Eve parties and later I saw you several times in the village and many times riding about the countryside on that roan."

Was he telling the truth? Had he really seen her that many times without her noticing him? Could he honestly have been smitten by her or was he just saying so now to try to make her feel more at ease?

His arm went around her and with his other hand he turned her face to his. "I can't believe that we are married," he said, "that you belong to me now." His lips played lightly over her face, stopping briefly on each eyelid, the tip of her nose and then her mouth where his kiss became more and more intense.

No! She could not allow this; her plan would be ruined if she let him go on.

So quickly that she almost pushed him off the love seat, Alexandra stood up. "Jason, I am tired, so tired I do not believe I can hold my eyes open another minute. Pray let me rest for a while."

He looked at her, first skeptically, then with concern. "Of course." He went to the bed and turned it down. "It is still early. Lie down for a while and I will join you later."

"Thank you." She did not trust herself to say anything else for fear of giving away her plan. He could join her later, but he would find her impossible to awaken.

After he left the room, she repacked her two portmanteaus, leaving out only the clothing she would wear tomorrow, then slipped out of her wrapper and got into the big bed. It was feathery comfortable and as soon as she lay down she realized she actually was as tired as she had pretended to be.

She had no notion of how much later it was, but she was awakened by movement on the bed. She opened her eyes and discovered Jason lying beside her, leaning on his elbow and studying her face. The only light in the room was from one lamp with a tiny, flickering candle on the marble-topped stand beside the bed.

She closed her eyes, pretending to go to sleep again immediately, but he trailed his finger across her face, under her chin, and then he was undoing the buttons of the high-necked nightgown. She gave what she trusted was a genuine-sounding yawn and tried to turn over, but his hand held her. Then his mouth was on hers and she pushed against him with all her strength before he finally raised his head and looked at her quizzically.

"Don't!" she gasped. "I must sleep. I am fatigued to death."

He gave what looked, in the lamplight, like a smile and proceeded to kiss her neck where he had unbuttoned the nightgown.

"I said for you to stop!" With a mighty push, she sat up, forgetting any pretense at sleep or sleepiness.

"But my dearest, this is our wedding night. What did you expect?" Those intense eyes of his seemed to be boring through her mind in an effort to read it.

"I expected you to behave like a gentleman," she declared.

He laughed as though she had said something tremendously amusing. "This *is* the way gentlemen behave on their wedding nights— and on other nights as well. Come now, Alexandra, you must . . ."

She sprang from the bed, snatching the green wrapper off the nearby chair. "You will not make love to me!" Her voice sounded louder than she had intended. "Not now or any other night."

He rose from the bed and stood before her, giving her a long, hard look. "What are you saying? What do you mean?"

She turned her eyes away from his nakedness and lowered her voice. "I have said *exactly* what I mean." She could feel rather than see his eyes burning into her like hot coals. "I will never let you make love to me."

Almost before she had finished speaking, he was putting on his clothes, and then he turned to leave the room.

"I do not want you ever to come near me," she added for emphasis, lest he think she was merely a timid bride who would be over her shyness by morning. "Remember that."

"I am not likely to forget, madam." He gave her the coldest look she had ever seen—she actually felt chills run over her body—and then he went out the door and closed it with a resounding bang.

She went back to bed emotionally exhausted, but she could not go back to sleep. She went over and over the scene in her mind, wondering if she could have done it differently so that they might have parted tomorrow without too much animosity. Finally, she fell into a light, troubled sleep.

The second time she was awakened, she heard the opening of the door. She lay very still, scarcely daring to breathe, as she heard Jason stumble against a chair. Next she heard him fumbling in the darkness, and then a lamp was lit and then another.

"I want to see my bride." He came to the bed and threw back the coverlet.

Alexandra sat up, clutching the sheet to her. "Get away from me," she hissed. Then, more in surprise than anger, she exclaimed, "Why, you are foxed!"

"I have had a mite to drink, madam." Standing beside the bed, he gave her a mock bow. "More than a mite, you might say. A mite more than a mite." He laughed as though he thought himself extremely clever.

To her horror, he began to remove his clothing, first his coat, then his blouse. "Don't you dare," she screeched. "Get out of here, you drunken rake!"

"You can't put me out of my own room, my pretty." He had now removed his breeches and continued disrobing methodically until his lean, hard body was completely exposed to her. She stared at his bulging manhood with mingled fascination and fear. With a grin she thought was satanic, he crawled into bed beside her, lunging for her as though he thought her a skittish animal that would try to escape.

"A man," he said, "is entitled to his wedding night."

She realized he was beyond reason. At first she tried to fight him, but he held both her hands in one of his and pressed her body against the bed so that it was impossible for her to move. He shifted just enough to strip her nightgown off over her head. Then, slowly, his free hand began to caress her at the same time that his lips found the tender spots on her throat and then her breasts. As his lips closed over first one breast and then the other and his tongue stimulated her sensitive nipples, she cried out, the new sensation making her almost wild. His kisses continued down her body, finally reaching the most secret part of her. She could not resist him any longer. Indeed, she did not want him to stop, and she responded to him as though she were a finely tuned instrument that could be played only by him. Her arms, which he had released, were around him now and she tried to pull him closer, closer to her while her own body strained upward to meet his. He entered her just when she thought she would scream with wanting him, and she gave a little gasp. The pain was instantly over and forgotten in the passion, hers equal to his. It was as though small ripples turned into waves that finally crested and became one huge tidal wave carrying them up, up, up in the sea of their desire. This, too, crested and broke, releasing them simultaneously.

They fell asleep in each other's arms.

She awakened to bright sunlight streaming through the window. She lay quietly in his arms, studying his face as he slept. Unlike the members of her family whom she had observed asleep, he did not have the look of a child. Indeed, there was nothing childlike about him. Even in sleep, his face had a decisive look.

In that instant she knew that he would always get what he wanted; he was that kind of man. He would take what he was entitled to, just as he had taken her. And she was glad that he . . .

Yes, admit it, she told herself; you loved making love with him. She would never stop wanting him now, and, realizing that, she also knew that she would never want any other man. She belonged to Jason now, heart, soul and body, for the rest of her life. It did not matter that she would never go to London to live among the wise and witty people. Jason more than made up for anything she might miss. Braley Acres was her home, Jason her husband. She could not get over the wonder of it.

Her arms tightened about him and he stirred. He opened his eyes and looked at her questioningly for a second, then he disengaged his arms from her and sat up.

"I don't suppose it would do any good to apologize for my . . . my actions last night," he said. "However, I shall do so anyway. You have my humblest, heartfelt . . ."

"Oh, Jason, that is not necessary," she said. "You do not have to . . ."

But he was not listening. He got out of bed and began to collect the clothing he had discarded on the floor, dressing as he picked up each piece. When he had finished, he turned to her. "You said you did not want me near you, and I assure you I would not have touched you had I not been besotted."

She stared at him, wondering what she could say that would take away his stern, unyielding expression and replace it with one of gentleness and love. She had thought that he had enjoyed their lovemaking as much as she. Could she have been wrong?

"I will make one confession, however," he went on. "Had I known you consider yourself untouchable, I never would have agreed to marry you." He laughed harshly. "Imagine Jason Braley, that devil with the ladies, taking a vow to wed but not to bed!"

It was true, then. He had tried her in bed

and found her wanting and he was telling her that it would be easy to let her alone from now on. What else could he be telling her?

"What do you mean 'agreed to marry' me?" she asked. "What kind of agreement?"

"The agreement with your father, of course," he said coldly. "My farmlands are not in the best condition and I needed a bit of blunt to straighten them out. Squire Coulter offered me an attractive sum to take you off his hands. Would you like to know just how much you are worth, sweet wife?"

She clapped her hands over her ears. "You are lying! I do not believe you!" Lemuel might ask someone to marry her, but he would never pay anyone to do so.

But deep inside, she knew Jason was telling the truth, and she hated him for hurting her with that knowledge, and she hated him even more for knowing that her father considered her no better than a piece of goods to be bought and sold. There was no thought of love now, only humiliation, a humiliation she would never forget, never get over.

At ten o'clock she had two of the footmen take her trunk and portmanteaus to the front hall. She neither noticed nor cared about the looks the footmen gave her and then each other, nor did she see the maids who peeked at her, sadly shook their heads, then went on about their work.

When Emerald arrived, fifteen minutes late, Alexandra flung herself into her aunt's arms, saying, "Oh, thank God you are here. I was afraid something had happened."

One look at the distraught face sent shivers down Emerald's spine. "What is it, child? What is wrong?"

"There can be no annulment," she said in a monotone. "I cannot get an annulment, it will have to be a divorce."

"No!" Emerald cried, backing away as though she had just caught a glimpse of Hades. "No, you cannot get a divorce. Oh, no, Alexandra, stop and think. You simply cannot *do* that. You would be ostracized for the rest of your life. You *cannot*, my dear. It is un*think*able!"

"There is no help for it," Alexandra said stoically, dry-eyed. "I must have a divorce."

Chapter One

THE AFTERNOON SHADOWS WERE LENGTHEN-
ing and a chill was in the air as the sun
dropped lower in the sky, leaving London
bathed in a peculiar pink and orange hue. In a
large house on Mount Street, Lord and Lady
Dysart sat before the huge stone fireplace of
their drawing room in companionable silence.
After thirty years of marriage, their closeness
was such that neither had to ask the other's
thoughts.

Lady Dysart was making the final plans for
the menu of an elegant supper they would
host two nights hence in honor of the Duke of
Melford. The duke had bought the house next
to theirs and had moved in scarcely a fortnight ago. Her ladyship felt it incumbent upon
them to entertain and become acquainted

with their new neighbor at once. They had called upon the duke and found him to be personable and engaging, and a bachelor living alone—and presumably lonely—in that big mausoleum of a house.

Lord Dysart was making plans for getting one man on the British throne and keeping another off it. That, of course, meant bringing the Pretender home from France and crowning him James III.

Both Lord and Lady Dysart started as a burning log divided and fell from the andirons. Evander rose from his chair, stirred up the fire with a poker, then put on another log from the brass bin. He was tall, gray-haired, with clear blue eyes.

"Do you need some help with the fire?" Monrovia asked.

He sat down again. "No, no, everything's fine. It was easier to do it myself." He looked at her fondly. She was a large woman, tall and big-boned, and her sandy hair was sprinkled with gray. She had been a beauty in her day, and to her husband she still was.

"I suppose it is easier for you to decide who is to succeed to the throne and take care of that matter yourself also," she said.

"How did you know what I was thinking?"

"Because that is all that has been on your mind lately."

He emitted a long sigh. "Something must needs be done and right soon. Anne's health deteriorates daily; she cannot last much longer."

"I have been hearing that ever since Prince George died five years ago," she said, "and still the Queen lives."

"I think the only thing that is keeping her alive is her conscience," he said. "She cannot decide which is better for England, to bring her half brother back as King or to let the rule go to the House of Hanover. She vacillates, often several times a day, I am told."

"But it is not up to her to say who her successor will be," Monrovia said. "That was decided by the Act of Settlement when she became Queen. If she and Prince George were to die childless, the throne would go to the House of Hanover." She gave her husband a steady look. "I do not know how you, or the Queen, hope to change that. Besides, Evander, has it not occurred to you that to bring back the Catholic James would mean a Protestant insurrection?"

Lord Dysart smiled. He was sure that he was the only man in London—nay, in all of England—with a wife who had a man's knowledge and love of politics and government. "It has occurred to everyone," he told her. "That is why we, those of us who want a Stuart, have been moving heaven and earth to get the Pretender to renounce Rome."

She gave a little laugh. "Perhaps heaven

does not want to be moved in matters of religion."

"Nor earth either, apparently," he said. "Viscount Bolingbroke, who was so positive he could sway James, failed completely. He told me only yesterday that he had had no conception of James's obstinate adherence to religion when it meant giving up all hope of the throne, which is what James has desired most of his life."

"Perhaps the viscount was not the right one to try to persuade James," she suggested.

"Bolingbroke is a brilliant man," her husband said, "but a trifle unstable. I have been thinking that it would be a good idea to send someone else to France to make one last effort."

"Who do you think could succeed where Bolingbroke failed?" she asked.

"It would have to be someone who has not been pestering James these many years to give up his religion," he said. "Someone James could respect—and listen to."

"Have you someone in mind?"

"I have been giving thought to the Duke of Melford."

"But you do not know him," she said, surprised. They had seen the duke but the one time.

"No, but I think I am a good judge of character, and I liked him on sight. As did you, I think, or you would not have suggested a supper in his honor."

"But suppose he is strong for the Hanoverians. Or suppose he really has no preference as to who ascends to the throne. Some people do not, you know."

He stood up, his back to the fire. "I shall not worry about that until after I have talked with the duke."

"Surely you're not going to ruin our supper with political talk."

"I shall wait until the ladies are not present," he said. "For that matter, I may take him into the library alone when we have our brandy. Which reminds me, isn't your sister coming for tea?"

"Ruthie is late, as usual. Shall I have Clemment bring in the tea tray before she gets here?"

"Please do. I am famished."

No sooner had she given the order to the butler than he came back to announce the arrival of Lady Lawring, who followed at his heels exclaiming, "So sorry I am late."

A birdlike woman with wispy gray hair and a nose not unlike a beak, she was all apologies. "Sorry, my dears, but you will forgive me when you hear what detained me."

"What?" Lord and Lady Dysart asked in unison.

"Could I trouble you for a cup of tea first?" she said, as Clemment rolled in the tea tray.

"And one of those delicious cakes. Rovie, remind me to get your cook's recipe sometime."

She bit into the little cake and smacked her lips. "Delicious!"

"The cake or the gossip?" Evander asked his sister-in-law. Although he did not actively dislike her, neither was he overly fond of her. Ruthie Lawring lived around the corner from her sister and brother-in-law in a house on Park Lane.

"Who said anything about gossip?" Ruthie asked.

"You have that look about you," Monrovia said. "We know you too well."

"It is not gossip, it is the truth."

"It can be gossip and still be true, for heaven's sake," Evander declared.

Ruthie smiled. "I have two choice morsels, actually. I'll save the real scandal until last. First—it is about your new neighbor, the Duke of Melford." She hesitated, but when neither of them spoke, she went on. "Nobody seemed to know anything about him except that he was not from London, but this afternoon I found out that he has more than a title and a big house on Mount Street. He has substantial holdings: not one, but *two* country estates. One somewhere near London and the other near the Scottish border."

His lordship suddenly was interested in the turn of the conversation. "What can you tell us about his political connections?" he asked.

His sister-in-law looked at him blankly. "Whatever would I know about that, Evander?"

Lord Dysart looked from her to his wife. How could sisters be so different? He gave a loud guffaw. "Then I take it your interest in his holdings stems from an ulterior motive. Are you setting your cap for a man young enough to be your son, Ruthie?"

"Evander, you sound like a Bedlamite!" Ruthie looked disgusted. "Rovie told me you both would like to know more about the duke before the supper you are giving for him, and I thought you would be glad to receive the information."

"Overjoyed," Lord Dysart murmured.

"From whom did you hear this?" Monrovia asked.

"Edward's nephew, Paul. I ran into him on Oxford Street. He was a schoolmate of the duke's at Cambridge and the two have seen each other from time to time. Oh, yes, and Paul said something quite strange. He said the duke does not like women of the gentility, only lightskirts and tavern wenches."

There was a moment of shocked silence, then Monrovia said, "Ruthie, do not be such an innocent! All men go through that phase. They call it sowing wild oats. Evander will bear me out."

Evander bore her out.

"If this is just a phase, then it has lasted for

46

a long time, I was told," Ruthie said, "and he has sown enough wild oats to feed the livestock on four continents."

Monrovia was thoughtful. "If his reputation is *that* tainted, perhaps we should call off the supper . . ."

"We will do no such thing," her husband interrupted.

Monrovia remained quiet as she poured second cups of tea for the three of them. Then she said, "I believe you had two bits of information to impart, Ruthie. What is the second?"

Ruthie had picked up her cup but she set it down without taking so much as a sip. "I have finally solved the mystery of Zandra Braley—or had it solved for me."

"What mystery?" Monrovia inquired. "I was unaware of any mystery."

"For nearly three years we have all been wondering about her," Ruthie said. "And now I know."

"Know what?" Monrovia's patience was not limitless.

"My dears," Ruthie looked from one to the other, "Mrs. Braley is not the widow we all took her to be—remember when she first came to London and we wondered why she was not in mourning, why she never mentioned a deceased husband? Well, Zandra Braley is—please do not faint when I tell you this—a *divorced woman*."

"Oh, my!" Monrovia leaned back in her chair.

"I always thought she was somebody's mistress," Lord Dysart said.

"If that's what you thought, why didn't you tell me?" Ruthie demanded. "You know that my son has taken an interest in her."

There was a benign smile on his lordship's face. "For all I knew, she could have been Gower's mistress."

"Evander!" Ruthie cried, too overcome to say more.

"He is only teasing you, dear," Monrovia said.

"How did you come by this sudden wealth of information?" Lord Dysart asked.

"From my friend, Isobel Mayhew. Remember her? She used to be married to that funny little man who bred horses and raced them at Newmarket. Well, she is Isobel Coulter now. I ran into her while I was shopping. It is the first time I have seen her in years. She married a squire who lives miles from here."

"What has she to do with Mrs. Braley?" Evander asked.

"Zandra Braley is Isobel's stepdaughter," Ruthie said. "Zandra married one of the local men a few weeks before Isobel and Squire Coulter married. Anyhow, it seems the marriage of the squire's daughter lasted scarcely longer than the ceremony itself. She sent for her aunt the *very next morning* and left her husband, bag and baggage."

"Which is what she sounds like," Monrovia commented, "a piece of baggage."

"Then she moved to London . . ." Lord Dysart prompted her.

"Not right away. She and Mrs. Wallace took rooms in Beaconsfield—Isobel said the squire refused to allow her back in the house, for which one cannot blame him—and they remained there for more than a year while Mrs. Braley obtained a bill of divorcement."

"So she was already divorced when she came to London," Monrovia mused.

"Yes, she came here passing herself off as a widow."

"Did she actually *say* she was a widow?" Lord Dysart asked.

"I don't know," Ruthie admitted. "Does it matter? She certainly gave that impression."

"Oh, my!" Monrovia exclaimed. "I just remembered—Gower has asked if he might bring her to the supper for the duke. We surely cannot allow a divorced woman . . ."

"And he is planning to bring her to tea with me tomorrow!" Ruthie said, almost screaming. "He asked me just today if he might. We will simply have to put an end to his acquaintance with that woman. Oh, Evander, you do not really think she could be his mistress, do you?"

Lord Dysart shrugged. "I don't know, but I can't fault Gower's taste. Mrs. Braley is a beautiful woman."

"And a divorced one," Monrovia said, still not entirely able to believe the shocking news. "How terrible!"

"Terrible that only royalty can divorce and still be socially acceptable," his lordship observed.

"Be that as it may," his wife replied, "we cannot allow Ruthie's son to become involved with a scandalous woman."

Chapter Two

AT THE MOMENT THAT SHE WAS BEING SO freely discussed, Zandra was awaiting the arrival of Gower Lawring, who was to take her for a walk in the park. He was late, and as the shadows lengthened, she began to think he would not come. It did not make a great deal of difference to her, but she had gone to the trouble to dress for him—in a lavender promenade gown of creped muslin—and she had not been out of the house all day, so she felt the walk would do her good.

She looked around the room to be sure it was in order; her one servant, Marie, was out for the afternoon. The small parlor, Zandra's favorite room, was cozy and informal and bright with color, rose and pink and red blending well in the draperies, the upholstery and the carpet.

She continued to stare out at the street, looking up occasionally as the shadows became deeper and deeper. Emma had gone out in the late morning for a day of shopping, including meeting someone she described only as "an acquaintance of old" for tea. Zandra herself had spent the day in a pensive mood.

The four years since her marriage to Jason Braley had been strange ones. After leaving the Braley house, she and Emma had taken rooms at the Beaconsfield Inn, and for nearly a week she had not left her room.

The reason she had not rushed at once to the nearest solicitor (and it was a long time before she would admit it to herself) was that she was waiting for Jason to come for her, apologize again for getting drunk on their wedding night and insist that she return to Braley Acres with him and be his wife until death, not divorce, did them part. That night with him, his tenderness when they were first alone together, the hours in his arms, half dreaming, half awake, his lovemaking were on her mind constantly, her first thought in the morning when she awakened, her last thought at night before she went to sleep. Even her dreams were filled with him, with his intense eyes looking at her with love, his hands caressing her . . .

After several weeks, it had become increasingly apparent to her that Jason Braley never wanted to see her again. One day she had inquired innocently of Emma, "Why do you suppose Jason has not even expressed a desire to know how I am? I could be ill, dying, for all he knows or cares."

Emma had given her a long look of disbelief. "I was unaware of your naiveté, my dear. I thought surely you knew what an untenable position you have put Jason in. You made him the laughingstock of the countryside. His bride left his bed and board without even unpacking her trunk."

Zandra had cringed at the words. She had never intended to hurt Jason or his pride. All she had been thinking about was how to get out of a forced marriage, how she could show her father that he could not make choices for her that she could better make for herself.

After that conversation, she was convinced that Jason despised her, and she became more and more despondent. Then she would remember that her father had paid Jason to take her off his hands.

She and Emma remained at the inn for more than a year, and not a day passed that Zandra did not hope that she might run into Jason on the street. During the time they were in Beaconsfield, Emma occasionally saw Lemuel and his new wife, but Zandra refused to go near either of them.

As time passed and she finally accepted the fact that Jason loathed her above all things, that he would never voluntarily be in her presence again, she said to Emma, "I am ready to see a solicitor now. Should I write a note to Jason to tell him what I plan?"

"You did not know?" Emma asked. "No, I suppose not. Lem told me some time ago that Jason left Braley Acres about a month after the wedding and has not returned."

"Where is he?"

"I don't know." Emma again tried to persuade her to leave Beaconsfield. "You're nearly twenty years old and you already have lost a year from your life sitting here. I haven't always thought that taking a house in London was the thing to do, but now I know it is the *only* thing to do."

The day after that conversation, Alexandra went to a solicitor and had divorce proceedings begun. When the divorce was a *fait accompli*, she and Emma left Beaconsfield for London.

The London she had dreamed about as an impressionable young girl and the London in which she lived as a divorced woman were two entirely different cities. The wise and witty people she had wanted to meet held forth at coffeehouses, but she never saw them. There were balls and suppers and parties to which she could never hope to be invited. What matter that she was stunningly beautiful and had gowns—those from her trousseau—the equal of London's finest? As a divorced woman there would not be even a modicum of acceptance in the Polite World if anyone should find out her true marital status, so she carefully avoided any situation in which questions would be asked of her. She was ever mindful of Emma's words to her on that fateful morning at Braley Acres: *No, you cannot get a divorce. You would be ostracized for the rest of your life.*

"We will tell people that I am a widow," she had said to Emma on their way to London.

"I don't think that is advisable," Emma had said. "You would have to tell other lies to make that one creditable, and someone is sure to find out the truth and expose you."

"Then we will say nothing at all and just let people assume that I am a widow," she had stated.

But there had been no way for them to make the right connections without revealing something of Zandra's "past." Finally Emma took matters into her own hands and looked up a former friend. She told her friend only that she and Zandra, her niece, "who is trying to put sad, really tragic, times behind her," had taken a house on Curzon Street and that Zandra had no friends of her own age in London. Emma's friend arranged a small supper party and Zandra was launched into at least a small segment of the Polite World. Her social ship soon went aground, however, for even though several of the young men begged leave to call upon her, she could manifest no interest in a single one of them.

The truth was, no man could ever compare with Jason Braley in her eyes. If only she could go back to the day of the wedding and relive that day and night differently!

How she had changed in the last four years! Alexandra Coulter and Zandra Braley were two entirely different people. Indeed, when she thought of the girl who had been Alexandra, it was like remembering vaguely someone she had known a long time ago.

Sometimes she and Emma went to the theater, sometimes to a concert, and that, for the most part, was her social life. Until Gower Lawring came along.

She had met Gower about a month ago while she was walking alone in the park. He had fallen into step beside her, causing her to stop and glare at him.

"Wait, please," he had said. "Don't walk away from me."

"You will leave me alone, sir, or I shall call for help."

He had gestured around at the crowded park. "Just the fact that so much help is readily available is reason enough for you not to call out. No, please don't turn away. I want to talk to you. I realize this is most irregular, but . . . You see, I have been watching you for the past week as you walked, and I wanted an introduction. I thought that you might stop and talk with someone who could introduce us but you have talked to no one."

He gave her a shy smile that she could not resist. It was impossible to be angry with someone so flattering and friendly. Besides, he was quite handsome with his tousled blond hair and twinkling blue eyes, and he had the manner and dress of the gentry.

"I am Gower Lawring," he said, "and you are . . . ?"

"Zandra Braley."

That was the beginning of the most satisfying friendship with a man Zandra had had since arriving in London, or ever, for that matter. The infatuation, however, was all on Gower's side.

She still thought obsessively about Jason even though she had tried to make herself hate him as he must hate her. Purposely she would repeat his words to her: *Had I known you consider yourself untouchable, I never would have agreed to marry you . . . Squire Coulter offered me an attractive sum to take you off his hands.* For a while, just thinking of those damning words would be enough to render her sane again. He was a despicable, money-grubbing rake and divorce had been too good for him; she should have considered murder.

But within five minutes, she was in his arms again . . . at least in her daydreams.

She heard carriage wheels approaching and looked down the street. Yes, it was Gower and he was driving himself.

She met him at the door. "It's late. Do you think we should start out now?"

"Probably not, and I apologize. I was detained because I had to do some errands for my mother."

"Perhaps tomorrow, or some other time," she suggested, disappointed that the walk had to be called off.

"Yes, tomorrow," he said, then looked beyond her. "Are you not going to invite me in?"

She shook her head. "I'm here alone. Even the maidservant is out for the afternoon."

He laughed. "My dear Zandra, one of the things I like best about you is that you have always seemed to know your own mind and have not followed the dictates of others. Now please let me in and offer me some refreshment, even if it is only tea."

She laughed also. "You're right. Come in. Will you take sherry, or maybe some claret?"

"Claret will do nicely," he said.

When she returned with two glasses of claret on a silver salver, he was standing in her former position by the window. He took the proffered glass, saluted her with it and drank. When she was seated, he sat down opposite her. "I have an invitation for you," he said.

"You told me of it nearly ten days ago," she reminded him. "We are to go to a supper at your aunt's in honor of the Duke of Melford on Thursday."

"No, I mean another invitation," he said. "My mother would like you to come to tea tomorrow afternoon."

She hesitated, wishing the invitation had included Emma as well.

"My mother is quite anxious to meet you," he added, as though this were a great inducement.

Finally she smiled and nodded. "Very well, though I fear your family will grow weary of me after seeing me on two successive days."

"Never!" he declared. "I will come for you at four."

"And our walk?"

"I forgot. Perhaps another time. My mother was quite insistent that I bring you to tea before Aunt Rovie's supper," he said. "By the way, don't let Uncle Evander frighten you when you meet him."

"Why should he?"

"He discusses little but the affairs of England and the succession to the throne these days."

"I shall be pleased to listen and learn from him."

He stood up. "I'm sorry I was late today, but I shall be here tomorrow promptly at four."

At the door he kissed her lightly on the cheek and said, "Until tomorrow."

After he had gone, Zandra leaned for a minute against the closed door. He was so nice, so kind to her, why could she not reciprocate? She did *like* him, but in the same way that she would like an affectionate child or a friendly puppy. It was not the way she would feel about a man she loved, not the way she felt about Jason.

Always Jason. Was there no way she could put him out of her mind, out of her life?

Gower Lawring was handsome, wealthy, of the nobility. And he was falling in love with her. Was she to spend the rest of her life in mourning for a future that had died before it had begun?

She had a feeling that Gower was going to offer for her hand in marriage—why else would his mother be summoning her? When he did, she was going to accept the proposal.

When Emma came home, Zandra would tell her that she was going to marry Gower Lawring.

All the way home in the hackney carriage, Emma tried to decide whether she should tell Zandra whom she had been with that day. By the time she reached the house on Curzon Street she had made up her mind. For four years now she had been treating her niece with velvet gloves because she knew the girl was still miserably in love with a man who rued the day he had ever heard the name Alexandra Coulter.

When she entered the small parlor she found her niece sitting in the large wing chair, so deep in thought that she did not hear Emma enter.

"Did your friend not come to take you for a walk in the park?" Emma asked.

Zandra started. "Oh, yes, Gower came, but he was late so we didn't go for a walk."

Emma sat down directly across from Zandra. "I met Isobel today and we spent several hours together," she said without preliminary.

"Isobel? Oh, Mrs. Mayhem," Zandra said disgustedly.

"Mrs. Coulter," Emma corrected. "I may as well tell you, Zandra, I have met Isobel and Lem several times since we came to London. Lem is my brother, and you cannot expect me never to see him again just because you wanted out of a marriage before you knew whether it would be enjoyable or lamentable."

"I recall that you were willing enough to help me get out of that marriage," Zandra said coolly.

For the first time, Emma wondered if Zandra blamed her for suggesting a means for ending the marriage and then helping her carry it out. "I was under the impression—mistaken, apparently—that that was what you wanted above all things."

Zandra looked away. "Let us not quarrel about it at this late date, Emma. What is done is done. How are Father and . . . that woman?"

"Both are well and, according to Isobel, both extend an invitation to us to visit at Coulter Manor whenever we would like."

"I think not," Zandra replied evenly.

"Your father would like to see you, Zandra," Emma said. "It has been four years . . ."

"I know very well how long it has been, and it will be even longer."

"You should not blame him for—"

"Not blame him for putting us out of our home? Then who, pray, should I blame?"

Emma clamped her lips together lest she say too much and break a promise she had made years ago.

"Aunt, the night before the wedding I heard you and Father talking and you were asking him to tell me the truth about something. What was it?"

"That is the first time you have called me Aunt in years."

"Do I get an answer?"

Emma waved the question away as though it were an annoying insect. "Whatever it was, it must not have been very important, for I have no memory of it at all now."

Zandra got up and was about to leave the room when she turned suddenly and said, "I'm to go with Gower to tea at his mother's tomorrow."

"I am delighted!"

"I think—that is, I have a feeling that Gower is going to propose marriage before very long and, Emma, I have made up my mind that I will go through with it."

You went through with marriage once before, Emma wanted to say, but what she said was, "Then you will be Lady Lawring." She did not add that asking for her hand in marriage and actually marrying her were two entirely different matters. It would hardly be possible for her to marry Gower Lawring without his first finding out that she was a divorced woman. Emma had a feeling that once he knew, what he proposed to Zandra would not be marriage. She could see nothing but more heartbreak ahead for the girl.

If only Jason Braley had not disappeared, she would go to him and demand that he see Zandra, for Emma was sure that if she could get the two of them together for even a few minutes everything that was wrong between them could be worked out. Jason had only to look into Zandra's eyes to see how much she loved him.

Chapter Three

"LORD LAWRING IS HERE, ZANDRA," EMMA called from the foot of the stairs.

Zandra gave herself one last inspection in the full-length mirror on the side of the clothespress. Was she suitably attired for her first meeting with the mother of the man she probably would marry? Yes, suitably, she thought, but certainly not in the last stare of fashion. She wore a pale green sprigged muslin that accentuated the color of her vividly green eyes; it had been one of the prettiest of her trousseau gowns . . . but a trousseau of four years ago.

That was one bit of knowledge—one of many bits—Lady Lawring, mercifully, could be spared.

She gave a little sigh, more of resignation than of sadness. Soon she herself would be Lady Lawring and Gower, Lord Lawring, would be constantly by her side. At home, away from home, everywhere, all the time. For the rest of her life. Fortunately, he was a pleasant companion, cheerful, thoughtful and with a real *tendre* for her. *Un*fortunately, he was not Jason Braley.

Quickly she tried to change the pattern her thoughts were forming by imagining herself as Gower's wife. She could visualize them everywhere together, except in bed. She imagined them on holidays at the coast, riding together in the park, attending small supper parties and large, formal balls. She could hear a butler announcing "Lord and Lady Lawring" to a great assemblage.

Lord and Lady Lawring. Mercy! It was like saying, "Let the last of the lions lie in the lair." Any poet worth his odes would shun such alliteration. But there was nothing poetic about the situation in which Zandra had found herself for the past four years.

She could, without too much difficulty, accustom herself to being Lady Lawring. It would be much better than being "that Braley woman" about whom part of London speculated and whom the rest of London ignored. Gower was rescuing her from the quagmire of questionable reputation. And rescuing Emma as well. It must have been hard on Emma these past years not to have circulated in the Polite World as she had done when she had lived in London before, hard to have lived on the fringe. Yet, Zandra wondered, was not Emma's life better here in London now than it would have been had she remained at Coulter Manor with Lemuel and the Mayhem?

With that thought firmly in mind she went, smiling, down the stairs to meet Gower.

The ride in Gower's carriage from Curzon Street to Lady Lawring's house on Park Lane was so short that there was scarcely time for an exchange of pleasantries, let alone a conversation. There was a slight chill in the air and Zandra shivered.

Gower immediately took her hand. "Don't be nervous," he said. "My mother quite looks forward to meeting you."

He had misinterpreted the shiver, but rather than tell him so, Zandra merely smiled. She could well imagine how Lady Lawring looked forward to meeting her . . . with a great deal of curiosity and, if Zandra were lucky, a smaller amount of animosity.

The carriage stopped in front of the imposing brick house that Zandra had passed so many times on her way to the park. She knew that this was where Gower had lived until he had taken rooms elsewhere, but today she looked at the house even more closely. It was huge. And it somehow bothered her practical nature to imagine such a large house being inhabited by only one woman—and a tremendous staff, no doubt.

Gower took her arm as they went up the steps to the massive front door adorned by two huge door-knockers in the shape of lions' heads. She gave a little shudder and was rewarded with an everything-will-be-all-right smile from Gower and a tightening of his grasp on her arm as though he expected her to bolt and run.

They were no sooner on the top step than the door was thrown open suddenly and an imperious butler in ornate black and silver livery looked down his nose at them from an imposing height.

"Good afternoon, Marius," Gower said. "My mother is expecting us."

"Good afternoon, sir, miss." He included Zandra in the greeting but did not so much as glance at her. "Her ladyship wishes to see you in her room, Lord Lawring, and asked that you join her immediately after you arrived. She wishes to see you alone," he added, as though afraid Zandra might assume that she was included in the summons.

They went inside to an entryway which opened onto a large reception hall. "Wait here, Zandra," Gower told her. "I suppose Mother has overslept and is not quite ready. She naps for a while every day." He bounded up the curving stairway on one side of the reception room.

Zandra elected to stand in the entryway rather than venture out into the larger room. She noted the appointments of the larger room, the Italian marble floor covered here and there by Persian rugs, the gold sconces liberally placed on all four walls, everything expensive and in good taste but cold-looking, like the room of a royal residence used only for state occasions. Her nervousness mounted and she almost giggled out loud. Never having been in a royal residence, how would she know what it was like?

Her eyes went to the one portrait on the east wall, a bewhiskered man with fair hair who bore a slight resemblance to Gower. Probably his father, the late Edward, Lord Lawring.

Minutes passed and she ran out of objects to study. What was taking so long? If Lady Lawring had overslept, why would she want her son present?

Zandra finally left the entryway and sat in one of the gilded chairs that lined the wall of the reception hall. At least fifteen minutes passed before Gower came slowly down the stairs, a slight frown on his face. She stood up and went to meet him.

"Mother has been taken ill," he said. "She extends her abject apologies and asks that the tea be postponed until she is in better health."

"Of course," Zandra said, almost relieved, though she knew the meeting would have to take place sooner or later. "I do hope it is nothing serious."

"A headache," he said, "which would be of little consequence except that I have never known her to have one before."

Zandra did not ask if *she* could be the cause of the headache, but the question was in her mind.

"I had better take you home now and then come back to see if there is anything I can do for Mother."

The frown remained on his face during the short drive back to Curzon Street and he said not a word. Zandra attributed his preoccupation to his mother's ill health and remained silent herself. In truth, she had been expecting an offer of marriage this afternoon which then would be announced to his family at his aunt's supper tomorrow night. But of course there would be no proposal when he was eager to get back to his ailing mother.

He walked her to the door of the small house. "I'll be here promptly at eight tomorrow to take you to the supper at my aunt's," he said.

"I will be ready," she said. "I hope you'll find your mother feeling better when you return."

He left her, almost running, and leapt into the carriage, which he had driven himself

69

this time rather than waiting to call his coach-man.

Zandra watched as he applied the whip to the pair and turned the corner as though he were off for the races at Newmarket. Such filial devotion was admirable . . . she supposed.

She entered the house thinking that tomorrow night would be the time. He would propose marriage to her then, either before or after the supper. A little smile played about her mouth as she wondered if he would be as solicitous toward his wife as he was toward his mother.

Gower left the carriage attended by a footman on the street and bounded into the house and up the stairs. He rapped lightly at the door of his mother's bedchamber lest she be asleep, then louder when he decided she must talk to him at once. There was much to be clarified, questions to be answered.

A maidservant opened the door and Gower asked if his mother could receive him.

"She is below, Lord Lawring, in the small sitting room having her tea."

Gower grimaced. It was as he had suspected. His mother did not wish to have tea with Zandra so she had feigned illness. He went down the stairs as he had come up them, two at a time.

There was a fire burning, making the small sitting room cozy. His mother, who had changed from her wrapper into an afternoon gown of French cambric, sat before the fire placidly holding her teacup.

"Well, Gower, I hardly expected you back so soon," she greeted him.

"If you had used your mind, you would have," he grumbled. "You can't leave me dangling as you did."

"I wasn't aware you were dangling." She took a sip of tea, the teacup momentarily hiding the beaked nose. "You seem to have both feet planted solidly on the floor."

"You know very well what I am referring to." He all but glared at her. "You cannot refuse to receive Miss Braley after saying that I might bring her to tea, and then not tell me why."

"I have every intention of telling you why, but not while she was cooling her heels below. I trust you have taken her back to wherever you fetched her from."

"You know very well that she and her aunt rent the Gunther house on Curzon Street." He was becoming more annoyed at every sentence his mother spoke. He had never before known her to do anything so rude as to refuse to see an invited guest.

"And I cannot, for the life of me, think what Iris Gunther had in her mind when she let the

71

house to that . . . that woman," Ruthie Lawring declared. "She must have been all about in her head."

Gower was astounded. "What could you possibly have against Miss Braley? You have never even *met* her."

"Sit down, Gower." His mother indicated a chair opposite hers, reached for the pot on the tea tray and poured him a cup. "To begin with, she is not *Miss* Braley but *Mrs.* Braley."

"You are misinformed," Gower told her. "I know everyone thought when Zandra first came to London that she was a widow, but she told me herself she is not."

"Better for her if she were." Her eyebrows raised in disapproval. "The girl you are so enamored of is a divorcée."

There was a moment of silence while a stunned Gower digested this bit of information. Then an explosion. "Of all the lying gossip I have ever heard, that takes *all* the prizes. Who is putting about such malicious nonsense?"

"It is God's truth and I heard it straight from the lips of *Mrs.* Braley's stepmother."

Gower set his cup back on the tray without taking so much as a sip. "I do not believe a word of it."

"Believe it," his mother told him.

"And furthermore, I have been planning—and still am—to offer for her."

"Not while there is breath in my body."

72

Ruthie Lawring grew as pale as the bone china teacup. "You will not disgrace this family by bringing scandal into it."

Gower only stared. It was as though the words that had been uttered in the room had been floating in the air, seeking a place to land, and had finally come to rest in his head.

"Another thing," his mother went on. "Rovie and Evander do not want you to bring that woman to the supper for the duke tomorrow night. Not only do they not want to entertain a pariah in their home, they also do not want to insult their new neighbor in whose honor the supper is being given."

Gower remained quiet for a long time. He could not, *did* not believe a word his mother had said. Somehow a terrible mistake had been made. He knew that for a while there had been a considerable amount of talk about Zandra—the two of them had laughed together about it only recently—but that was because she never talked about herself and everyone had been busy guessing at or making up a past for her. She always had been the soul of propriety with him—and didn't the fact that her aunt, Mrs. Wallace, lived with her as chaperon prove that she was exactly what he thought: a proper, well-brought-up young woman?

When he spoke, his voice was firm and his decision inflexible. "I shall take her to the supper tomorrow night, or . . ." There was the tiniest pause. "Or I shall stay away myself . . . permanently."

"Gower, what are you saying?" his mother cried. "You're talking nonsense. You must know—"

"I know that I am adamant and nothing you can say will change my mind." He stood up quickly. "I shall go tell Aunt Rovie right now that if Zandra is not welcomed tomorrow night, she and Uncle Evander have seen the last of me."

He hurried out of the room and out of the house before his mother could answer, slowing his steps only when he reached the street. He shook his head as the footman moved to help him into the carriage, telling the man he would not be needing it as he was only going around the corner to the Dysart residence.

He walked even more slowly once he had turned the corner and was out of sight of his mother's house. Was there even the slightest possibility that the gossip his mother had heard could be true? Could Zandra have . . . No, of course not! Zandra herself had told him shortly after they met that she was not a widow though she knew that "the loose tongues of the busybodies are saying that I am. The truth is . . . I have no husband." Nor family either, he had surmised, except for the aunt. That eliminated a stepmother, wicked or otherwise, for surely Zandra would at some time have mentioned her father if he were still living. Or, just possibly, there *was* a stepmother who had been jealous of Zandra while her father was alive and was now trying to ruin her reputation.

He gritted his teeth. Malicious, gossiping women! He would settle the whole thing tomorrow night by asking Zandra the truth of the matter. Meanwhile, he would have to prevail upon his aunt and uncle to admit Zandra to their supper.

"Good afternoon, Clemment," he greeted the butler who answered his knock. "Is my aunt at home?"

"Good afternoon, your lordship." Clemment bowed formally. "Lady Dysart is out, but Lord Dysart is in the library. May I announce you?"

Gower pushed past the butler, enroute to the library, and said, "I shall announce myself."

He found Evander Dysart leaning against the high mantel over the fireplace in the library, his forehead furrowed as though he were deep in thought.

"Good afternoon, sir," Gower said, hesitating at the door. "I hope I am not interrupting you."

Lord Dysart turned slowly to face the younger man. "As you can see, I am standing here in total idleness."

"But you seem to have weighty matters on your mind." Gower took a few steps backward, thinking this might not be the best of times to give the stern-looking peer an ultimatum. "I came by to see Aunt Rovie, but Clemment tells me she is out."

"Running thither and yon seeing to something about tomorrow's supper, I think." Lord Dysart shrugged. "I do not try to keep up with the domestic part of the arrangements. Come in, my boy. You may as well have a few words with me now that you are here."

Gower joined Lord Dysart in front of the fireplace. His lordship indicated that they both should sit down, then said, "Anything in particular on your mind, Gower?"

Gower hesitated, then said, "Well, yes there is. I understand that you and Aunt Rovie are against my bringing Zandra Braley to the supper tomorrow night."

"Both Monrovia and your mother think it would not be quite the thing," he said, "but as for me . . ." He gave a wink. "As for me, I find the young woman pleasing to look at, as do other men, I'm sure."

Gower winced. "It isn't like that, Uncle. She isn't *that* kind of woman. She is the soul of propriety." He repeated what he had said to his mother. "As for this gossip about her being divorced, I am sure it is just that: gossip."

"As far as I am concerned, you may bring whomever you wish to the supper," Lord Dysart said, "as long as you can square it with your mother and aunt. *They* are the social arbiters of the family."

Gower sighed with relief. "If they know it is all right with you, then it will be all right with them." His mission accomplished, he rose to go.

"Is that all you wanted?" Lord Dysart asked, motioning for Gower to sit down again. "As long as you're here, you may as well stay and visit. You come seldom enough. Shall I have Clemment bring tea, or something stronger?"

"No, thank you, Uncle. I was hesitant about staying because you seemed to have something on your mind when I came in."

Lord Dysart nodded. "I was thinking about the terrible muddle that even the keenest minds are in right now. Sometimes the question of succession can cause more trouble than the wrong monarch after he attains the throne."

Gower, an ardent Jacobite, sat back down immediately. He was firmly among those who wanted to keep a Stuart on the throne by bringing the Pretender back to England and crowning him James III upon Anne's death.

"Have there been developments of which I am unaware?" he asked.

"No, no, nothing new," Lord Dysart said. "I spoke with Bolingbroke again yesterday. The viscount is more eager than ever to find someone who can convince the Pretender to renounce his religion, since that is the main obstacle standing between him and the throne."

Gower jumped up again and paced about the room. "Oh, how I wish I might have a try at persuading James. I believe—no, I am *sure* —that I could prevail."

Lord Dysart waved the idea away as though unworthy of consideration. "Gower, even as Jacobites go, I sometimes think you are over-zealous."

"Then I am the very one to send to France," Gower said. "Surely the viscount would not delegate such a herculean task to one who is only lukewarm about the issue."

"I told Bolingbroke yesterday that I have someone in mind to send for one last try at changing James's mind," Dysart said. "I am much impressed with our new neighbor, the Duke of Melford. If he can be talked into going, I believe he would have no difficulty getting James at least to listen to his suggestions."

"Talked into going!" Gower could not believe he had heard aright. "If he has to be talked into it himself, then he surely will not be able to persuade James of anything, least of all into giving up or changing his religion."

"I will find out exactly how the duke stands tomorrow night," his lordship said. "If he is not of a mind to go, then I suppose Bolingbroke himself will try it once more."

"And we will have a second failure on our hands," Gower muttered. "Uncle, you *must* send me! You have a great deal of influence with the viscount. Please, I beg of you . . ." ·

"Save your breath, Gower. I myself do not believe it would be wise to send you to France, therefore I cannot in good conscience recommend you to Bolingbroke." Lord Dysart stared at the younger man as though assessing him anew. "You have youth and verve on your side, but I think perhaps we need someone with a cooler head and an ability to argue using reason rather than rabidity."

Gower's face reddened with anger. "What you're saying is that you don't want to send a boy to do a man's work. Well, I can assure you . . ."

"Let's talk about something else, Gower," Lord Dysart said gently. "I think we have exhausted that topic. Now, about the Braley woman—"

"I do not like hearing the lady of my choice referred to in that manner!" The slight only added to Gower's agitation.

"I do beg your pardon," Dysart said with a rueful smile. "I was unaware she is a lady."

"Maybe not by title, but certainly by every other way of judging," Gower said grudgingly.

"By all means bring her tomorrow night," the older man conceded. "It will help to make for a lively evening."

Gower prepared to take his leave. "I hope you will inform Aunt Rovie that Zandra is to be here, so that she will not look or act shocked when we arrive together."

Out on the street again, his mind was in turmoil but his uncle's implied insults to Zandra were forgotten. He was thinking again of Evander's refusal to send him to France to talk to James. If *he* could be the one to persuade the Pretender to renounce Rome, to sign whatever papers were necessary to bring him back to England as King, then the name of Gower Lawring would be known throughout the country and Europe as well; he would go down in history as the man responsible for keeping a Stuart on the throne.

He stopped suddenly, looked toward the heavens and made a solemn vow. If necessary, he would move heaven and earth to be the one to go.

Chapter Four

ZANDRA SAT AT THE VANITY TABLE IN THE small dressing room off her bedchamber, staring at the face in the mirror as though at a stranger. There was nothing familiar in the pale, thin face with the wide mouth that seemed unable to smile even though tonight was likely to be an occasion to bring a smile to the lips of any marriage-minded miss. Even the dark-fringed, deep green eyes seemed like the eyes of someone she had never seen before, some poor, haunted soul she would be better off not knowing.

She was dressed in the best of her trousseau gowns, a silver-green, moiré-patterned faille trimmed with ivory soutache. She had never had occasion to wear it before.

Thinking about her trousseau made the tiny

frown on her face increase slightly. Quickly she pinched color into her cheeks and stood up. She did not want to look at the stranger in the mirror any longer or discover what that haunted girl was thinking. It was a waste of time to think of all that now; there was nothing that could be done about the past. She went downstairs as soon as her toilette was finished.

"I have never seen you look more beautiful," was Emma's first comment.

"Truly?" Zandra asked, surprised. "I have never seen me look more haggard." She went to the front window and drew back the curtain so she could look out.

"It isn't seemly to appear so eager," Emma reminded her.

Zandra smiled for the first time, but made no reply. Gower's carriage had just stopped in front of the house.

Though she had attended several social functions—a ball or two, a reception, a tea—also attended by Lord and Lady Dysart and Lady Lawring, she had never been presented to them. Tonight she would take on Gower's entire family.

With resignation she stepped through the front door of the Mount Street mansion and was shown into a large salon that occupied the south side of the ground floor. Gower gripped her elbow firmly and steered her toward a small group by a refreshment table.

He stopped before a tall, big-boned woman whose sandy hair was sprinkled with gray and whose expression changed as she looked at Zandra. Her pleasant smile faded, but Zandra was not sure what expression replaced it.

"Aunt Rovie, may I present . . . Zandra Braley?" Gower hesitated. At the last minute he had been unsure whether to introduce Zandra as Miss or Mrs., so he compromised by omitting the title altogether.

Zandra, not sure whether she should curtsy, bowed her head deeply as Gower continued the introduction. "Zandra, my aunt, Lady Dysart. And my uncle, Lord Dysart."

Lady Dysart nodded to Zandra but said nothing. His lordship, however, bowed and said, "We are pleased to welcome a friend of Gower's."

"Thank you," Zandra murmured, wondering how to carry on the conversation.

"Where is Mother?" Gower asked. "Oh, I see her over there. Excuse us, please. I must present Zandra." He was leading her across the room before she could think of anything to say to Lord and Lady Dysart.

"Mother, may I present Zandra Braley?" he said. "Zandra, my mother, Lady Lawring."

Again Zandra inclined her head deeply. "I

am pleased to meet you, Lady Lawring, and more than pleased that you have recovered sufficiently from your illness of yesterday to be here tonight."

"Indeed." Lady Lawring's beak of a nose was tilted upward at a somewhat awkward angle and her half-closed eyes were hooded like a hawk's. "Zandra," she murmured. "What kind of name is that?"

"I was christened Alexandra."

"I should hope so." Now the eyes were opened wide. "Excuse me, I see my sister motioning to me. I must help her and Lord Dysart greet their guests." And she was on her way across the room without another word or glance in Zandra's direction.

Zandra started to question Gower about the cool reception she had received, but hesitated. She said instead, "That is a lovely gown your mother is wearing," and noted even as she said it that the olive satin gown heavily brocaded with roses seemed to be wearing the woman instead of vice versa.

Gower smiled, pleased. "Yes," he said, "Mother prides herself on her impeccable taste in everything, clothing especially."

Too bad she doesn't pride herself on good manners, Zandra wanted to reply but, again, held her tongue. "Do you suppose we could have a glass of wine?" she asked.

Back at the refreshment table, Gower directed a footman to pour each of them a glass of claret, then introduced Zandra to the rest of the guests. With each introduction, she felt more and more uncomfortable. No one volunteered to engage her in conversation beyond a perfunctory "How do you do?" and she had the distinct feeling that as each guest passed on to another group, she was the object of surreptitious glances. At one point, she could have sworn there were even whispers emanating from one small group on the other side of the table. She took several swallows of wine and held out her glass to be refilled. "How long will this last?" she asked Gower.

"The doors to the dining parlor will be opened shortly and we will go in to supper," he said, then added, "Hmmm, I don't see the guest of honor. Certainly he must have arrived by now." He looked around the room and also missed his uncle. "Oh, I suppose Uncle has cornered him and is talking politics."

"Yes, I had forgotten. The supper is for a duke, I think you said."

"The Duke of Melford," Gower said. "He has just recently become a neighbor."

Something about his tone made Zandra suspect that the duke did not rank very high in Gower's esteem. "He is not a friend of yours, I take it," she said.

"I've never met him," he said, "though I confess I am eager to. It will be interesting to see what kind of man could have made so great an impression upon my uncle on such short acquaintance. Here, give me your glass. I'll get more wine."

The object of the conversation in the salon was at that minute behind the closed door of the library. Evander Dysart had spotted the duke the moment Clemment had appeared in the doorway with His Grace at his heels, and he had hastened across the room to greet him, at the same time propelling him toward the library.

"Before we join the others, Your Grace, there is a matter of some urgency that I would like to discuss with you."

Puzzled, the duke had watched as his host turned the key in the door. For a moment or two they had discussed the unseasonably chilly weather. Then, without preamble, Evander said, "Sir, I would like to know whether you are a Whig or a Tory."

The duke's strange, magnetic eyes seemed to stare right through Lord Dysart. He was thoughtful for a moment, and then replied, "I'm not committed either way. I believe I lean more toward the Tories, however, since I am more often in favor of the crown than Parliament."

His host nodded as though pleased with this reply, then asked, "And the Queen? How do you feel about her?"

The duke drew himself up to his full height of well over six feet. "I feel that Anne is a much better queen than she is given credit for being. I have a great deal of contempt for those who disparage her with the name 'Brandy Nan.' May I inquire as to why I am being questioned along this line?"

"I probably should have told you before I began the inquisition," Evander said with a smile. "But I wanted to know first . . ." Then he began his prepared discourse about Viscount Bolingbroke's desire to try one more time to convince the Pretender to renounce Rome and come back to rule Protestant England. "We both think that what is needed is someone who is persuasive yet not overzealous," he said. "The first time I saw you, I took you to be a practical, down-to-earth man, the perfect model of what we are seeking . . . if you are desirous of keeping a Stuart on the throne, that is."

"You wish *me* to go to France on this errand?" the duke asked, surprise showing plainly on his face. He ran a hand through his thick, dark hair.

"Exactly. But only if you are convinced that James should come back to seek the crown."

The duke was silent for a long time, his dark brows knit together in thought. Finally, he spoke solemnly.

"I have never been absolutely certain that the Pretender is the legitimate heir of James II and Mary of Modena."

Evander nodded. "I am sure I have heard

every version of the story that James was smuggled into the queen's bedchamber in a warming pan. At first I had my doubts, too. But now I am certain the Pretender is indeed a Stuart."

"How can you be so sure?" the duke asked.

"Because he bears a striking resemblance to Charles II, both in looks and in gait. I was with Bolingbroke when he first went to St. Germain and I saw James then. There was no doubt in my mind, on seeing him, that the warming-pan story was false—at least no baby was brought into the palace in that pan. The young James is truly a Stuart."

"I confess I do not like all I have heard about the House of Hanover," the duke said slowly, "and since we have fared rather well under the Stuarts, I would rather see one remain on the throne."

Evander nodded. "My sentiments exactly. Then may I count on you to go to France for us?"

The duke hesitated. "I have never been much involved in politics, nor do I care to be."

"I promise you that you need not involve yourself any more than merely to talk to young James," Evander said. "Previously, we have sent old men who tried to play on his sympathy and his patriotism—and he put his religion ahead of both. Now I would like to try someone nearer his own age who will appeal to his reason. You cannot be more than a few years older than he, and you seem to be a *most* reasonable man."

The duke smiled ruefully. "How can I refuse when baited with such flattery?"

"Then you will go?"

"Yes. But I cannot promise you any more success than you have had from the others."

So great was the relief that flooded through Evander that he almost sagged in his chair. "All we ask is that you try," he said.

As the evening wore on, Zandra's eyes went frequently to the tall, gilded clock in one corner of the vast salon. It seemed impossible that she had only been here for an hour. Surely the clock must have stopped. She and Gower had moved about the room, stopping to talk with first one little group and then another. In each case, the introductions were acknowledged and everyone listened politely when Zandra talked, but no one ever addressed a remark to her. She had consumed more wine than she ever had before at one time, yet she felt no effect whatever. She knew that the longer she had to remain in this house under the disapproving eyes of the ladies Dysart and Lawring, the more uncomfortable she would become.

Most of the guests were older than she and Gower except for one young lady, a Miss Cordelia Finch. When they were introduced, she had stared at Zandra as though Zandra had done her some terrible wrong, and it was only later, after catching the girl eyeing her several times, that Zandra realized that the wrong she had done was to take Gower away from the girl.

Cordelia Finch was more than attractive, with blond hair that cascaded in waves to her shoulders, big blue eyes that looked as though they belonged in a china doll, and dimples that only accentuated her china-doll look. As Gower and Zandra went from group to group, they almost invariably were joined by Miss Finch.

Now, as the clock struck nine, Zandra and Gower stood alone near one of the floor-to-ceiling windows.

"We shall be going in to supper soon," Gower said for the fourth time in twenty minutes.

"I hope you are right," Zandra replied in a tone just this side of civil. "Frankly, I have about given up on getting sustenance."

"It is customary to allow an hour before supper for conviviality," Gower said, his own tone of voice a few degrees cooler, letting Zandra know that he did not like any criticism of his family, no matter how veiled. He cocked his head. "Ah, I see my uncle approaching. That means Uncle has had his little talk with the duke and supper can be served now."

"For small mercies, let us be thankful," Zandra murmured as she saw Lord Dysart, followed by a taller man, enter the room. The guest of honor was partially hidden behind his lordship. Lady Dysart immediately motioned to Miss Finch, who was presented to His Grace. The girl bobbed a curtsy and took the duke's arm just as Clemment opened the double doors leading into the dining parlor and announced in magisterial tones, "Ladies and gentlemen, supper is served."

Zandra, on Gower's arm, arrived at the double doors simultaneously with Lord and Lady Dysart and the duke and Miss Finch. Lord Dysart began to make the introductions, but Zandra heard not a word—she was staring unabashedly at the guest of honor. A little gasp escaped her lips. The Duke of Melford was her ex-husband, Jason Braley.

Chapter Five

GOWER FROWNED SLIGHTLY AT ZANDRA. WHAT
had come over her so suddenly? Her face was
chalky white and he could feel her trembling
on his arm. Had she been stricken with an
attack of the vapors, or was it something more
serious? Then he glanced toward the duke
and saw that he, also, had paled and was
returning Zandra's stare.

Somewhat unsettled by the strong reaction
between the two, Gower asked innocently,
"Have you met before?"

"Only briefly," Zandra replied, then
clamped her lips together.

"At a wedding, I believe," the duke said.
The tension seemed to be lifting and Gower
was almost sure he saw a twinkle in those
strange, penetrating eyes.

When Zandra said nothing, the duke continued, "I seem to remember becoming a little better acquainted following the ceremony. Perhaps you remember, ma'am, it was several hours after . . ."

"I do not remember!" Zandra said emphatically.

"How odd that you have met before," Lady Dysart chimed in, her tone indicating that she could not quite take in this coincidence. "Perhaps if you can recall whose wedding it was . . ."

The duke shrugged. "It was not a very important wedding. In fact, it was of no significance whatever."

"He is absolutely right," Zandra agreed. "It is best left forgotten." Her heart was pounding so rapidly she was afraid she would faint, and that she *must* not do. Above all things, she must not let Jason know how much seeing him again had affected her, he who was standing there as cool as winter's coldest day, looking at her as though she were some curio being thrust upon him against his will.

Cordelia Finch, on the duke's arm, began to fidget. "Shall we go in to supper?" she said. "I am sure Lady Dysart would prefer we continue the conversation at table instead of blocking the doorway." She gave Zandra a long look that said plainly, "You may have taken Gower from me but you will not get *this* one."

"There is nothing more to say," Zandra murmured.

"Yes," the duke agreed heartily. "By all means, let us progress from here to the next . . . room."

He hesitated over the last word just long enough to make Zandra catch her breath. The scoundrel! The abysmal, hellhounding, villainous scoundrel! He was thoroughly enjoying the situation and her discomfiture. Oh, if only she could embarrass him, make him squirm, make him rue the day he had moved into a house beside the relatives of her intended . . . Oh, dear Lord, she thought. Jason was living next door to the Dysarts and she undoubtedly would run into him at every supper party, ball, reception, tea and rout after she and Gower were married.

But there was no time to think about that now. Gower was urging her into the dining parlor and one of the footmen was seating them at the long banquet table.

"There must be some mistake," Gower whispered to her after she was seated. "I will speak to my aunt. We have been put below the salt."

"Do not say one word to her," Zandra said between clenched teeth, noting with relief the distance between her and Jason. "We will stay right here."

Clearly disgruntled, Gower sat down beside

her. At the head of the table, Lady Dysart sat with Jason on her right, and seated next to him was Cordelia Finch. To the right of Lord Dysart was Lady Lawring, and thereafter the guests were seated according to title and importance. Except for Gower, of course. It was because of her, Zandra knew, that Gower had been given one of the less favored seats. But that thought was of no consequence whatever right now.

She could not keep her eyes from repeatedly turning toward the head of the table, but not once did she catch Jason looking at her, surreptitiously or otherwise. He had changed little in the four years since she had seen him. The thick, dark hair still had a somewhat unruly look and his eyes their ability to see right through a person. His face was fuller, but he had not entirely lost that shrewd, calculating look.

As Zandra watched, he signaled the wine steward to pour more wine for Miss Finch, then put his head close to her ear and whispered something to her. Something that delighted her, obviously, for she threw back her mane of blond waves and laughed merrily.

Zandra found herself gritting her teeth and resenting every attention Jason showed the girl. But why should she care? He was no longer her husband, and it should not upset her if he was unduly attentive to another woman. No, she didn't mind at all; for all she cared, Jason could flirt openly with every woman in the room.

By the end of the sumptuous meal, she could not have told what had been served, what she had eaten, in what conversations she had engaged, or even who sat on her right. She was aware of only one thing—Jason Braley's nearness.

What had happened to him in the last four years when he had ostensibly disappeared from the face of the earth? How had the squire from Beaconsfield become a duke?

A new type of wine was brought in with dessert and Zandra almost started when Jason stood up and raised his glass. "Ladies and gentlemen, I give you . . . the good health of the Queen."

"To Queen Anne," was murmured around the table as everyone drank. The host and hostess were toasted next, and then the talk returned to the subject of the Queen.

"Her health is atrocious," Lord Dysart said. "The wonder is that she is still alive."

"With heaven's mercy, she will live long enough to change the Act of Settlement so we can bring the Pretender back," said a man about halfway down the table.

"I don't think she will change it, even if she lives," Dysart said. "And Parliament certainly won't approve. Most of the peers are for the House of Hanover."

Lady Dysart rose. "If you gentlemen want your politics, brandy and cigars here at the table, we ladies will repair to the drawing room."

"No more politics," Lord Dysart said, also rising. "We will *all* go to the drawing room."

"Good." His spouse nodded her approval. "Cordelia has agreed to entertain us at the pianoforte."

The evening wore on interminably. Cordelia, a mediocre musician, assaulted their ears with her playing for a good twenty minutes and then for another ten minutes sang to her own accompaniment. Compared with her singing, Zandra decided, her playing was that of a virtuoso.

Once again, Zandra's eyes strayed constantly to Jason, while his eyes never left the purveyor of the evening's entertainment. Finally, when there was a short break to allow the songbird to catch her breath, Zandra whispered to Gower, "I have a terrible headache. Do you mind if we leave?"

On the way back to Curzon Street, Gower looked at her intently. "Is the headache the reason you were so quiet all night?" he asked.

"Yes," Zandra said, "it came on me suddenly."

"Right after you met the Duke of Melford, I take it."

"I don't remember exactly when." She tried to sound nonchalant.

"There seems to be bad blood between the two of you," Gower remarked.

"There is no blood at all between us. Nothing!" She was aware that she said it too vehemently.

Gower helped her from the carriage and walked her to the front door of her house. "I hope your headache is better," he said. "If I may, I will call on you tomorrow to find out."

She nodded, bade him good night, and went inside. So engrossed was she in thoughts of Jason that it did not occur to her until much later that Gower had said good night . . . without proposing marriage to her.

Jason bade his host and hostess good night with many thanks for the elaborate supper given in his honor, and then, as custom required, he escorted Miss Cordelia Finch to her home on Brook Street, all but insulting her by leaving her at her door with no mention of a future encounter. The truth was that he thought her a silly, vain little thing and didn't care if he ever saw her again. But the *greater* truth was that Alexandra was so much on his mind that he was scarcely aware that another woman inhabited the earth. When he returned to his house on Mount Street, he alit like a somnambulist, went dazedly into the house and made straight to the library. He poured himself a double brandy, sat down in his favorite wing chair, unlaced his boots and put his feet up on a footstool.

Even this comfort did not ease the pain in his mind.

Why did she hate him so? From the very first she had loathed and despised him, and he did not have a glimmer of an idea why. He had felt nothing but love for her, had shown her nothing but love.

He had told her the truth when he said he had wanted her from the first time he saw her. He could still see her as she had been that day in the village, her long auburn hair ruffled by a gentle wind, her mobile, interesting face a study of . . . what? She had always had a quality he could not define, something that was completely lacking in other women of his acquaintance. There was more than beauty in that face, there was character, strong character. (And who should know better than he *how* strong?)

He had hoped to woo and wed her in the normal way, but she would have none of it . . . which should not have surprised him much after the conversation with her father. That visit should have forewarned him that theirs would not be a normal courtship.

He remembered how nervous he had been the day he went to Squire Coulter to ask permission to call upon his daughter. The squire had looked him straight in the eye and said, "May I ask your intentions?"

"I hope to win her heart and marry her, sir," Jason had said unhesitatingly. Silly expression, "win her heart," but it would hardly do to say to the girl's father on the first visit that he hoped to make her want him with as much fire and passion as he wanted her. He could not tell Squire Coulter about the long restless nights he had lain awake, aching with the desire to make love to the older man's daughter.

"Good!" the squire exclaimed immediately. "How soon would you like to marry her?"

The question caught Jason so unawares that for a moment he could only stare in wonderment. "As soon as she will have me, sir," he said finally.

"The sooner the better," Squire Coulter said, and then they had made what Jason considered the strangest deal he had ever been involved in.

Jason had lost track of how many nights he had sat, just as he sat now, with feet up and brandy in hand, pondering on the wedding and the wedding night. The four years that had passed since then had not dimmed a single memory, had not diminished one whit the ache in his heart . . . nor, for that matter, his hurt pride.

He would always remember how devastated

he had been when Alexandra, visibly cringing, told him not to come near her. It had not been an attack of bride's nerves; no, it was much more than that. She knew—and had conveyed to him—that whatever it was that caused her complete antipathy toward him would last a lifetime. Had she not told him she *never* wanted him to touch her? Never is a lifetime, an eternity.

He had done everything he could to change her mind, even thinking—foolishly—that once initiated into the rites of love, she would lose that strange aversion to him.

The following morning he had tried again, beginning by apologizing for his actions of the night before, though how she could misinterpret his love for her was something that eluded him then, and now. His apology had only aroused more anger and abhorrence on her part. And then she had left Braley Acres with all her possessions, making him the butt of bad jokes throughout the countryside.

It was not to be endured: the behind-the-hand snickers of the servant girls, the sympathy in the eyes of the older male servants, the remarks—meant to be amusing but hurtful instead—of his peers.

A few days after Alexandra's flight, Squire Coulter had gone to Braley Acres and offered to forget the "deal" he and Jason had made, but Jason had informed him grimly that he would not go back on his word even though the squire's daughter seemed to have some difficulty in keeping hers.

Finally, unable to stand the looks, the sympathy, the remarks and the advice, he quit Braley Acres for his uncle's estate near the Scottish border.

His father's older brother, Zachariah Braley, the Duke of Melford, was sick with lung fever when Jason arrived and it was obvious that, even if he recovered, he would never again be able to manage his large estate without help, preferably from someone who would not cheat him—as the duke's overseer had been doing for the past two years. So Jason took over, as delighted to have something to take his mind off his own troubles as his uncle was to have someone he trusted take over the management of his holdings.

He heard nothing from or about his wife until a year later, when he received a letter from his solicitor in Beaconsfield saying that Alexandra Coulter Braley had sought and obtained a bill of divorcement from Jason Wilton Braley.

Shortly after he received the letter his uncle again took a turn for the worse and never recovered. Unmarried and childless, the duke left all of his holdings and his title to Jason, who decided to remain at Melford Manor, going back to the Beaconsfield estate only rarely to see how it prospered under the overseer who ran it for him.

His existence was a solitary one. His nearest neighbors were almost ten miles away and his only companions were the household staff and the men who worked his fields. Only recently, tired of nothing but work and his own company, he had bought the house in London, thinking to make some kind of new life for himself. He knew he should meet people, become a sociable being again, and eventually think of producing heirs for his vast holdings . . . though every time the thought of marriage crept into his mind, he thrust it away as something to consider later, not now.

Always later, because not a day had gone by in the past four years that Alexandra had not occupied his mind, his soul, his whole being, even though he never expected to see her again. It was with difficulty that he admitted to himself that even when he had bought the Mount Street house, he had had Alexandra in mind. Was it a house she would like? How would she decorate it, furnish it?

Seeing her at the supper tonight had stunned him; for a moment he had felt as though the world had dropped away, leaving him suspended in space. And then when he had recovered his equilibrium, his heart had taken flight and in one split second he had imagined every sort of favorable outcome possible from the evening. But Zandra had snubbed him entirely.

Turning his brandy snifter around and around in his hand, he asked himself again the question that had obsessed him all these years: why did she hate him so? When they had made love, that one night of their marriage, she had seemed to enjoy it; her passion had matched his. Why, then, could she not bear the sight of him?

He would never have any peace of mind, never rest easy, until he found the answer to that question. Finishing the brandy in gulps instead of sips, he vowed he would find out—and soon. He would make it a point to see Zandra again.

Chapter Six

ZANDRA POURED HER SECOND CUP OF COFFEE, then set it down without taking a sip. She looked across the breakfast table at her aunt, thinking that Emma looked as tired as she felt herself. Since Emma had not waited up for her last night, Zandra had assumed that her aunt had been asleep, but judging from the circles beneath Emma's eyes, she too had lain awake long hours counting the strokes of the clock every hour.

When Zandra had come downstairs, she had found Emma sitting down to breakfast. Emma greeted her expectantly. "Tell me all about the supper party—and the evening."

Zandra gave a long, detailed account of what she could remember of the supper, the entertainment, the people there, but neglecting to reveal the identity of the Duke of Melford. When her recital was finished, Emma continued to look at her questioningly.

"I came home with a headache," she began.

"Is that the way you describe the man you intend to marry?" Emma said with a smile.

Zandra returned a pathetic half-smile. "Gower did not propose last night because I was not feeling quite the thing, but he is coming here today . . ." She let the words trail off, still wondering what she would say to Gower when he did propose. All night she had thought about Jason and what seeing him again had done to her. Could she possibly marry another man knowing that Jason would be foremost in her mind for as long as she lived? On the other hand, look what seeing her again had done to him! His friendly smile of greeting had turned to a sour expression as soon as he recognized her, and every word he had spoken to her had dripped sarcasm.

Marry Gower, a little voice within her said. When you are safely married to him, there will be no more scenes like last night's. You will be Lady Lawring, accepted by the Polite World, and Jason will not be able to bother you anymore with his cutting remarks. Besides, you really are *quite* fond of Gower . . .

"Aunt, you could never imagine who the

guest of honor was last night," she said suddenly.

"The Duke of Melford, I think you said," Emma replied.

"The Duke of Melford is Jason Braley."

Emma sucked in her breath in surprise, but before she could answer, the front doorknocker sounded.

Marie, their cook-housekeeper-maid, entered the breakfast parlor and addressed Zandra. "It is Lord Lawring to see you, ma'am."

"So early," Zandra murmured, then remembered that she had been late in rising. "Show him into the small sitting room, Marie, and tell him I will join him shortly." She turned to Emma. "Am I suitably gowned for receiving an offer of marriage or should I change into something else?"

Emma nodded approvingly at the sea green crepe. "You might overdo it if you change." As Zandra left the breakfast parlor, Emma wondered once again whether Gower really planned to marry Zandra. Somehow she could not imagine his mother approving his marriage to a woman about whom so little was known and so much was speculated in the inner circles of the social world.

Gower was sitting bolt upright in the most uncomfortable straight chair in the room. He stood up when Zandra entered. Without so much as a "good morning," he said at once, "I must ask you something."

What a monstrous hurry he was in, she thought, not even to inquire about the state of her health, which had been the reason for his not being able to ask that question last night.

"I am feeling much better this morning, thank you," she said tartly.

"I am glad because I must ask you something," he repeated. He paused only briefly, then asked, "Is it true that you have been married, and that you divorced your husband?"

Zandra, stunned by the unexpected question, plopped into the nearest chair. Only then did Gower resume his seat and stare at her intently. She stared back, no answer coming readily to her mind. If Gower, and others, knew about the divorce, they could only have found out from Jason.

"That man should run his mouth in the marathon," she said softly. "It would win, hands down."

"*What* are you talking about?" Gower asked, mystified.

"I suppose he has told all of London."

"He who?"

"The Duke of Melford, of course," she said. "I thought you knew. He is the man I was married to."

Now it was Gower's turn to be stupefied. His

mouth opened but no words came out. He made a few inarticulate sounds, then finally managed to say, "I should have guessed from your actions last night." There was another long silence, then he added, "But whyever did you divorce him?"

"Because I never wanted to marry him in the first place," she told him. "I was forced into it by my father."

Gower gave a long sigh.

"Is *that* the question you interrupted my breakfast to ask?" These long silences were making her uncomfortable.

"Yes, no . . . I . . ." Now Gower inhaled deeply. "Zandra, you know how . . . how, er, fond of you I am . . ."

"I hope I do, Gower," she said softly. Everything was all right now; he had recovered from his initial shock and he was about to propose.

"Yes, well . . . I would like . . . would like to offer you . . . a *carte blanche!*"

"A . . . what?" She looked at him, uncomprehending.

"A *carte blanche*. You know, you can name your own terms, anything you want. I will set you up in a beautiful house, or rooms in a fashionable place, or even take over the financial upkeep of this house if that is what you prefer. And, of course, if you are set on it, your aunt may stay with you as long as she does not interfere in any way . . ."

"What are you *saying*?" Zandra could not believe she was hearing correctly. "You are making it sound as though you are asking me to be your *mistress*."

Gower smiled benignly, delighted that Zandra had caught on so quickly without his having to go into every little detail. But then, her quick mind and sharp wit were two of the qualities that most strongly attracted him. "Exactly," he said. "I think we would deal extremely well together, don't you?"

Zandra surveyed her immediate surroundings quickly, looking for a vase, a trinket, anything she could hurl at that smug, smiling face. Finding nothing, she rose, took two steps to his chair and slapped him so smartly across the cheek that her fingers stung. Then she resumed her seat and stared at him stonily.

He rubbed his cheek and then looked at his hand as if he expected to find blood there. He stood up as though to leave but walked to the other side of the room instead. "Is that your answer to my very generous offer?"

"It is." Zandra could not even bear to look at him now; she fixed her eyes upon a painting of a stormy landscape on the far wall. "It was not the offer I was expecting."

"Not what you expected?" For a minute he did not understand, then he said, "Surely you were not expecting an offer of *marriage*?"

Zandra nodded, still without looking at him. "I thought you were an honorable man and I expected an honorable offer of marriage."

Gower sat down across from her again. "To be truthful," he said, "it was in my mind at one time to ask you to be my wife, but naturally, in view of your divorce, that is impossible."

She turned her head and looked him straight in the eye. "I am exactly the same person I was yesterday, a week ago, a year ago! I have not changed in the slightest, and if you thought me worthy of being your wife then, why not now?" Not that she would marry him now if he begged her on bended knee, but she wanted him to see the fallacy, the sheer idiocy, of his thinking.

He could not meet her eyes, looking down instead at the mauve Persian rug. "Perhaps I am the one who changed," he offered, "when I learned that you are a *divorced woman*."

"You make it sound as though I have a loathsome disease," she said disgustedly.

"Just think if I were to marry you, Zandra," he burst out. "Neither of us would be received in any decent home in London, not even my own mother's. We would be ostracized!"

"So! In the space of a few hours, I have become a fallen woman. A woman to be used as a mistress, but never taken for a wife."

Gower moved to the back of her chair and put his hand lightly on her shoulder. "We could have a grand time together, Zandra. Think about it! You would never have to worry about anything, ever again. I would love you so . . . and always take care of you. Why, I'd give you anything you want, *everything* you want."

Zandra smiled sadly. He was more like an immature boy than a man of the world who would take a mistress. Odd that she had not seen this side of him in the months of their acquaintance. "You would give me anything I want . . . except respectability. Is that it, Gower?"

"You must know that that is not within my power," he said. "When you divorced your husband, you made yourself an object of scandal. You made your own bed, and now you must lie in it."

"But I do not have to lie in yours."

He reddened slightly. "Please, Zandra. All I ask right now is that you think about it. As I said, I am quite fond of you. In fact, I think I . . . I am quite in love with you. Now there! I have never before said that to any woman. You can see that marriage is impossible between us, but love is more than possible, it is—"

"If I remember my history correctly," she interrupted, "a King of England remarried following a divorce."

Gower nodded. "Yes, my dear, but we are not talking about royalty."

Zandra stood up, went to the door and opened it. "If you are still of a mind to give me anything I want, then you will leave this house at once and never come back. I never want to see you again."

He walked slowly to the door. "Will you not even think about my offer?"

"I have already given more thought—and conversation—to it than it deserved," she said.

"But if you will give yourself time to get used to the idea, I am sure you will . . ."

"Time is what you need, not I." She gave him a frosty look. "When icebergs from the realms of hell come up and puncture the ground, I will become your mistress."

He went out the door, and she slammed it so hard that the beams in the ceiling of the room shuddered. She waited until she heard him driving away in his carriage before she left the room and went up to her bedchamber.

She sat down on the side of her bed and noticed that her hands were trembling, as they always did when she lost her temper. But Gower's proposal was hardly worth a second thought, much less losing her temper over.

She sat very still for a long time. She felt as though the center of her emotions were paralyzed. Surely she should feel anger or sorrow, or *something*. The truth was, she now realized, that Gower meant so little to her that she could feel nothing at all, not even a minute's disappointment that he had not proposed what she had been expecting.

All she could think about was Jason . . . and how much she wanted to see him again.

Gower stomped to his carriage, the sound of the slammed door reverberating in his ears like cannon fire. He had always thought Zandra a passionate, high-spirited woman, but he had never expected her passion to be spent on him in *this* way. Unpredictable spitfire! His cheek still burned and he would wager the print of her hand was clearly discernible on his face. He should have thrown her across his lap and given her the beating he would have given any unmanageable, obstinate child. He should, even now, be cursing her for the dissolute woman of scandal she was. But he had never wanted her more. He actually felt pain in his loins for want of her.

Curtly he dismissed his coachman, telling the man to walk home, that he wanted to go for a drive by himself.

He jumped onto the box, took the whip to the pair, and set out from Curzon Street as though he were off to put out a fire. Which, he thought grimly, was just what he was trying to do, put out the fire that raged in him like a hellish conflagration. He hurtled around Hyde Park Corner, the carriage precariously balanced on two wheels, and proceeded down Knightsbridge, whipping the pair on. Never in his life had he felt such extreme anger.

What he wanted to do more than anything

on earth was to turn the carriage around, go straight back to Curzon Street and offer Zandra marriage . . . if she would have him now. But he knew that he could not do it, could *never* offer her more than he already had. He had been completely right when he told her they would be ostracized by respectable London. For that matter, he was of the opinion that even the riffraff of London would look askance at a lord marrying a woman of scandal. Somehow Zandra had managed to keep her divorce a secret for three years, but that secret was out now, and he would hazard a guess that by nightfall it would be all over town. Only gossip could travel faster than an out-of-control fire.

But, dear God, how he wanted her! Why, *why* wouldn't she be reasonable and accept his offer? Any other woman in her position would have walked hot cobblestones barefoot for the chance. Maybe that was why he wanted her so, because she was not like any other woman.

His anger surged up anew, but this time it was not directed at Zandra. He suddenly realized that the cause of his wrath, the cause of *all* his frustrations lately, was not Zandra but her former husband, the Duke of Melford. The duke, who had come out of nowhere onto the London scene like a comet dropping from the heavens, was ruining his life. First, the duke had married the woman Gower himself wanted to marry, thereby making it impossible for Gower to consider her. As if that weren't enough, the duke had insinuated himself into Lord Dysart's notice so that Gower's own uncle chose Melford for the honor that Gower craved most in the world.

It was not to be endured!

Somehow, some way, Gower was going to turn everything back around the way it was supposed to be. The way it had been before the duke arrived. Gower finally turned the carriage around. All the way back into town he plotted and planned. *He* would be the one to bring the Pretender back from France to the throne of England. And that accomplished, he would take Zandra as his mistress—and he would have her begging him for the honor!

Chapter Seven

JASON PROWLED FROM ROOM TO ROOM IN HIS newly acquired mansion. Although he had had some furniture sent from Melford Manor and Braley Acres, he had supplied himself with only the necessities. It had been his thought to have one of the fashionable Oxford Street decorators furnish the house, but lately he had had so many other things on his mind that the empty rooms seemed of secondary importance. His library and his bedchamber were completely furnished and had that look of having been long lived in. Also, he had taken care to see that the servants' quarters were comfortable.

As he paced, his mind went over and over his meeting with Zandra three nights ago. Every word she had said to him, every look he vividly remembered, but there was no way he could read more into any of it than he had on that night, when she had made it perfectly obvious that she would have preferred to go the rest of her life without seeing him again.

He had tried, unsuccessfully, to think of some reason he might have to call on her, but he knew that she would refuse to see him even if he came up with the best of excuses. It seemed that his only hope was to encounter her again at another social function. He wondered if she visited the Dysart house often, but he supposed that whether she did or not would depend on how much she saw of Lord Lawring, Lady Dysart's nephew. Just how close were she and Lord Lawring?

Of course! Why had he not thought of it before? Except for the principals, who better could fill him in on the details than Lord and Lady Dysart? And he had the perfect excuse to call on them. It had been three days since the supper in his honor and he had not yet made his obligatory call to thank them.

He sent a footman to the Dysart residence at once to ask if it would be convenient for him to call. The footman returned with the message that Lady Dysart was visiting at the home of her sister, Lady Lawring, but that Lord Dysart was in and would be delighted to see the duke.

Jason would have preferred that Lady Dysart be present, for he was sure she could come closer to telling him what he wanted to know about Zandra and Lord Lawring, but he could not very well postpone the visit now. He was admitted to the house next door by Clemment, who showed him into the drawing room.

"Afternoon, Your Grace," his lordship greeted Jason. "What will you have? A brandy, perhaps?"

"Yes, if you'll join me." Jason extended his hand. "And please, since we are neighbors, let us not stand on such formality. My name is Jason."

"And I am Evander. Odd, but I don't believe I have heard your full name before. What is your family name?"

"Braley," Jason said.

"Braley," Lord Dysart repeated. "It is not an uncommon name in this part of England."

Jason waited to see if Dysart would make the connection between his name and Zandra's, but apparently the older man had more pressing things on his mind, for he said at once, "I am glad you came by today, otherwise I might have sought you out. I am to see Bolingbroke tomorrow morning and we shall discuss your journey to France. I think you should get under way before winter sets in proper. Also before the Queen's health fails entirely."

"Is her condition worse?" Jason asked, taking a snifter from the silver tray Clemment held.

"It has gone from worse to worst," Dysart said. "I do wonder if there is any truth in the rumor that she is deep in her cups morning, noon and night."

"I think her drinking has been exaggerated —as are most stories connected with royalty," Jason said, "but I would not be surprised if she took a nip from time to time." He raised the snifter and saluted his host.

Dysart smiled, the gesture not lost on him. "It is no secret, however, that when Prince George was alive the two of them enjoyed imbibing together. It is no wonder if she has continued, poor thing. Opinion about her has crested and fallen, like a ship on high seas, ever since the day she became Queen. The truth is, she was no sooner crowned than the rumors began that George of Hanover was being touted for king, even though he had rejected Anne as a suitor years before."

"Tell me about the Pretender," Jason said. "I know nothing about him except what one hears in the streets."

"James Francis Edward Stuart." Dysart murmured the name as though repeating a litany. "In France he is called the Chevalier de St. George."

"Well thought of by the French king, I understand," Jason said.

"I am not sure how well thought of," Dysart said, "but it would be very much to Louis's advantage to have James on the English throne."

Jason nodded. "And of course, James did make a try for it a few years back."

"Five years ago," Dysart said. "He was twenty years old at the time, and he took a fleet of ships to Dunkirk, ready to sail for Scotland, set up court and declare himself King of Scotland. When news of this spread throughout England, the people immediately stopped their divisive wrangling and were solidly behind Anne. It was then, I think, that Anne fully understood that the throne was not his by divine right, but hers by the will of the people."

"And now she is about to die and the will of the people once more is divided," Jason said.

The older man nodded. "Only last year the Whigs tried to convince Marlborough to force the Queen to abdicate and put the House of Hanover on the throne."

Jason stared reflectively across the room. "I have one very serious reservation about helping to re-establish the Pretender as king," he said. "If James comes back to England, I fear there will be a Protestant insurrection that will end in bloodletting."

"Not if he comes back as a Protestant," Dysart said, "or at least in sympathy with the

Protestants and with a signed declaration that he will not persecute them."

Jason paused thoughtfully. "I must confess to you, Lord Dysart, that I have very little hope of succeeding where others have failed," he admitted. "If Viscount Bolingbroke and God knows how many others could not talk James into renouncing his religion, I have no reason to believe I can."

Dysart nodded. "It is understood that if you fail, you fail, and there is no help for it. But I have every confidence in you, Jason. Only old men have tried before, and those who could gain personally by James's return. You are not doing this for your own advantage, but for the good of the country; you are a reasonable man and a persuasive one. You are, in other words, our last and best hope."

"I will try," Jason said, then repeated softly, "I will try."

For a moment the two men were silent, slowly sipping their brandy. The subject of the Pretender had been exhausted, as far as Jason was concerned, and he was trying to think of some way to bring the conversation around to what he had come to discuss. Finally he said, "I appreciate more than I can tell you the welcome I have received from you and Lady Dysart. The supper party in my honor was most gracious of you."

"Our pleasure. Monrovia is never so happy as when entertaining."

"I was glad for the opportunity of meeting her nephew, Lord Lawring."

"Oh—Gower." Dysart laughed. "Whenever I hear Lord Lawring, I think instantly of Gower's father, Edward. We did not rub along too well together."

"His son seems a pleasant enough fellow," Jason persisted.

Dysart shrugged. "I suppose so, but he has his faults, God knows. I am strong for the Stuarts, as you know, but Gower is positively *rabid*. An overzealous Jacobite, if you ask me."

The talk was straying off course, Jason thought. "The lady with him," he said. "He seemed most attentive to her. Is there to be an announcement soon—or has there already been one?"

Dysart laughed again. "Not while the world turns. His mother and my wife will move heaven and earth to prevent it. You see, the woman with him is no lady. She is a divorcée."

Jason bristled. "That I should know better than anyone. I am the man she divorced. But believe me, sir, that does not preclude her being a lady!"

"Oh, my God! Braley." Dysart was dumbfounded as the name registered in his mind. He coughed, cleared his throat, coughed again, then said, "I do apologize, Jason, if I have offended you. I did not know . . ."

"You had no way of knowing," Jason said, his anger dissolving as quickly as it had arisen.

"We only found out about her divorce a few days ago," Dysart said, "in spite of the fact that she has lived in London for some years. I think everyone took it for granted that she was a widow."

"I had no idea whether it was generally known or not," Jason said. "If it is not, then I hope you will keep my confidence. If the *lady*," he accentuated the word, "does not wish it known that she was once married to me, then I should not like to be the one to make it known."

"You can count on me to keep my lips firmly sealed," Dysart smiled. "*I* would not like to be the one to give the gossipers more fuel for their fires. I think . . ."

His thought was interrupted by Clemment, who appeared at the door to announce Lord Lawring. The words were hardly out of his mouth before Gower strode into the room saying, "Uncle, I *must* talk to you at once—Oh!" He broke off on seeing Jason.

The two glared at each other as Jason rose from his chair.

"I was not aware that you had a visitor," Gower said, his cold stare never leaving Jason.

Jason smiled—irritatingly, he hoped—and

said, "I was just leaving, your lordship. Thank you again, Lord Dysart. And will you tell Lady Dysart how sorry I am to have missed her?"

The older man nodded. "I will indeed. But I wish you would stay. I am sure that whatever Gower has to say is not in the nature of a state secret." He looked to Gower for confirmation, but Gower did not speak.

"I have stayed longer than I ought to as it is," Jason insisted. "No, do not get up. Clemment will see me out."

Outside, the thought of going back to the nearly empty house—empty in so many ways—was repugnant to him. The afternoon shadows were lengthening and there was a chill in the air, but the park a block and a half down the street looked inviting. He would go for a brisk walk before going home to his solitary meal.

It was growing late and she knew she should go home, but Zandra, whose nerves had been on edge ever since the Dysarts' supper, found relief only in constant movement. In the house she tried to stay busy at something every minute: helping Marie about the house, chatting animatedly with Emma. But no matter how she tried to occupy her mind, she still could not forget the misery of the past few days. So in spite of the cold and the approaching dusk, she had flung on her cloak and left the house, unable to find any other tasks that needed doing.

Heading for the park, Zandra thought about her aunt's behavior during the past few days. After Gower had left the other morning, Zandra had not had to say a word to Emma about what had transpired. Emma had seemed to know, as though by some sixth sense. After several hours, when Emma had not asked a single question, Zandra had said merely, "He did not propose."

"Not marriage, perhaps, but I suspect he proposed something," Emma had said.

How could she have known? Zandra had felt too wretched to pursue the subject then, nor had she wanted to broach it since. But she knew she could count on Emma for cheerfulness and understanding without fearing an inquisition.

She drew her cloak tighter about her. It was really cold now; she had had no business coming out. She should have stayed inside by the cheery fire and had a glass of wine with Emma. She turned and started back in the direction from which she had come, but she had gone only a few steps before she heard footsteps behind her. She slowed, thinking the person behind her would want to pass on the path, but the footsteps behind her slowed also. She walked faster again and so did her follower. A little alarmed, for there was no one else about in the park, she turned and then stopped short in surprise.

"Why are you following me?" Her tone was as ungracious as she could make it.

"Because I want to talk to you," Jason said.

"I told you the other night we have nothing to say to each other. How long have you been following me?"

He smiled. "Only since you turned and started back this way. Until then, I wasn't sure it was you."

"Well, now you know, and you can go back whatever way you came."

"Please, Zandra—see what an apt pupil I am; I used your new name—please, let us talk." He looked at her imploringly.

"About what?"

He did not answer. Instead he took her arm and looked deeply into her eyes. She could not meet his gaze for long; she knew that if she did, he would know exactly what she was thinking, know that she was drowning in that magnetic stare, being pulled down by a powerful undertow.

"You are trembling," he said. "It is much too cold for you to be out. Besides, it will be dark before long. Do you live near here?"

She pointed. "I live over there. On Curzon Street."

He looked surprised, and she knew he was thinking of their proximity, only six blocks apart. "Come," he said, tightening his grip on her arm, "I am taking you home—and then we will talk."

She said nothing because there was nothing to say. She did not want to send him on his way. Nor did she want to let him know how eager she really was for his company. Just the thought that he wanted to talk to *her* caused her heart to pound wildly. Anxiously, she wondered if all he wanted was to make recriminations, to upbraid her unmercifully for leaving his home, for divorcing him . . . for so many things she now considered the height of folly, even stupidity, on her part.

She stopped suddenly as they reached the street. "I think it would be best if we said good-bye right here."

He propelled her almost roughly along the walk. "Oh no, my dear former wife, for once you are going to face the music. You are not going to slip away like a child who behaves irresponsibly and then hides from the consequences. Now which is your house?"

Jason marched her in the direction she indicated and rapped loudly on the door.

"I did not think you would stay out long—Oh!" Emma swung open the door, her eyes wide with surprise on recognizing Jason. Recovering, she said quickly, "Come in, Squire Bra—I mean, Your Grace."

Jason bowed to Emma. "Just call me Jason,

please. We were, after all, related by marriage."

"Yes, my nephew-in-law," Emma smiled. "Once removed."

Jason laughed and said, "Almost twice removed, but not quite. Not yet."

They all went into the small sitting room and Emma said, "Sit down, Jason, and I will bring wine. Or would you prefer something stronger?"

"I will have whatever Zandra has," he said, leaving Zandra wishing she could be as at ease as he.

"Wine," she said softly, sinking into the nearest chair.

Jason sat down in a chair opposite hers. Emma returned with a silver tray bearing two glasses and a decanter of wine which she set on a table beside Zandra. Then, making her excuses, she left the room hastily.

"There is a woman of sensitivity," Jason said. "I am sorry we are not still related by marriage."

Zandra poured the wine, using that as an excuse for not answering, rose and handed him a glass. Jason raised his glass in salute to her, took a sip, then said, "Well, are you not going to say one word?"

She sat down again. "It was you who wanted to talk."

"So it was." He took another sip of wine.

Then he smiled at her. "But it is not as easy as I thought it would be."

Zandra began to fidget under his burning gaze. Finally, to break the silence that was almost like a third presence in the room, she said, "It was a very nice supper party the other night. Had you met Lord and Lady Dysart before you moved next door to them?"

"Zandra, why did you leave me the morning after we were married?" he asked abruptly. "Why did you divorce me without giving our marriage a chance, without giving me the opportunity to show you—"

Zandra set her glass down sharply on the table, spilling a few drops. "Show me!" she interrupted. "You showed me enough. More than enough! You showed me what it was to have a heartless, unfeeling husband. Why, you were almost a stranger to me, and what did you do on our wedding night but drink yourself into such a state of inebriation that it might as well have been a bacchanalian festival! And then you raped me and—"

"Wait a minute!" Jason held up his hand. "Just a minute. Did my lovemaking seem that of a drunken man? The only drinking I did that night, I did with you. I was completely sober, but I needed some excuse to get back into your bed. If you remember, you said some unexpected—as well as unkind—things to me that night. You told me you did not want me to touch you, ever. I thought I could change your mind about me by making love to you, and making you think that I was besotted was the only way I could think of to get back into bed with you. Did my lovemaking seem like that of a drunken man?" he asked again.

"How would I have known?" she answered. "I had nothing, or no one, with whom to compare you." Her voice was softer now and she was no longer glaring at him.

"Why did you reject me before you gave me a chance to show you how much I loved you?" His eyes burned into her again, daring her not to tell the truth, promising dire consequences if she lied.

"You loved me?" She could not keep the amazement out of her voice. "No, I do not believe it. You accepted money from my father to marry me. You told me so the morning after."

"I lied to you," he said, his voice so low now that she had to lean forward to hear him. "My pride was near mortally wounded and I wanted yours to be also. Your father did not pay me to marry you, not a farthing. I was the one—" He broke off suddenly, looking away from her. She could tell there was a struggle going on inside him over whether to reveal some long-hidden secret.

"Tell me, Jason." But no, she did not want him to make up some lie on the spot that would attempt to excuse his inexcusable behavior of that night. "No, never mind, I don't want to hear it. I *know* my father paid you to marry me because I know the circumstances. Emma knows also, though she won't go into detail about it. She has never denied that Father paid you, so it must be true."

"Your aunt was probably pledged to secrecy," Jason suggested. "All right, Zandra, I will tell you the truth."

Suddenly she was afraid to hear what he was going to say. She knew that after Jason had spoken, her life would never be the same again.

"If you promised not to tell, perhaps you had better keep your word," she said.

"I will not be breaking my word," he said quickly. "I was released from that promise a few days after you left Braley Acres. Your father came and . . . Well, I shall start from the beginning."

He hesitated for still another long minute and when he spoke his voice was low, almost inaudible. "Our marriage was not your father's idea, it was mine. I was the one who asked him for your hand. You see, I had been in love with you since the first day I saw you. Well, I went to him and asked permission to call upon you. He asked my intentions, as any father would, and I told him I wanted to marry you." He had been staring down at his hands in his lap while he talked, but now he raised his eyes, meeting hers. "Your father informed me that the sooner we were married, the better, but that there would be no dowry. I am sure you know that he had had two very bad years: crop failures, disease among the livestock. He was so much in debt that he was in fear of losing the estate."

Zandra gasped. She had known that things had gone abominably on the farm for a long time, but Lemuel had kept the worst of it hidden from her.

"He told me that in order to save his land, his home, he had agreed to marry a woman who had been, in his words, 'wanting to make a marriage for a long time.' This woman, he said, would pay off most of his debts, thus enabling him to plant new crops and buy more livestock. In other words, almost have a fresh beginning. I told him I would take on his debt, and that there was no need for him to marry unless he wanted to. He said it was a matter of honor, for he already had made the arrangements with the lady. There was only one thing standing in the way: you and your aunt. The lady did not want either of you living at Coulter Manor when she came there as mistress.

"I told your father that I would be delighted to take you both, that Braley Acres had been too long without a woman and that to have two such charming ones would be a double honor. I also—" He looked down at his hands again as though about to confess something shameful. "I also gave your father the money he needed so that he would not have to remain totally in debt to his wife for the rest of his life. He made me promise that I would not tell you, for he thought it would look as though he were selling you to me."

Zandra's eyes were wide with astonishment. "Instead, I thought he had paid you to take me off his hands. Is that not just as bad?"

"That was my fault," Jason said. "I am sorry to have hurt you so, Zandra. You had hurt me, so I . . . But that is no excuse. I never should have lied to you."

"And I should never have given you reason to lie," she said. "Oh, Jason, there is no way to count the times I have regretted leaving you, or the times I have wished I could turn the calendar back to the day of our wedding." Tears welled in her eyes as she looked at him. "Did you mean it when you said you had always loved me?"

"I cannot remember a time when you were not the center of my world," he said. "Even after you left me and I thought I despised you for what you had done to me, I still loved you. Not a day has passed since then that you have not been in my thoughts. Even when I bought the house here in London, I could picture no woman in it but you. I have spent my days wondering how you would decorate the house, what piece of furniture you would put here, and there, how beautiful you would look descending that curved staircase."

"Oh, Jason," she breathed, unable to say

more. And then she gave him a smile so radiant that it resembled a glorious sunrise.

He looked at her wonderingly for a minute, and then he arose from his chair and knelt by hers, taking her in his arms. His mouth was upon hers instantly in a scalding kiss that was almost painful in its intensity. Then her arms were around him and she was returning his kisses feverishly. They embraced desperately as though trying to devour each other, to make up for a long fast, to assuage all the want and longing of the past four years.

Finally, he held her at arm's length and asked, "Why, Zandra, why?"

She knew at once what he was asking. "It was not *you* I was rebelling against," she told him. "I was furious at being forced to marry someone I did not know. I had been promised a season in London and like a child I was sulking because that promise was not being kept. I had no way of knowing that my father couldn't afford a season at home, let alone one in London." She gave a little laugh, and her voice dropped lower. "Also, I had always dreamed—ever since I was a little girl—of marrying a man I loved completely and absolutely, a great love that would last a lifetime." She lowered her eyes and said softly, "I did not know, until too late, that you were that love."

Wordless, overcome with emotion, he took her in his arms again, holding her close, stroking the lovely auburn hair. She nestled against him like a traveler who has been on a long, weary journey and has finally come home.

"Zandra," he said after a long pause, "will you be my wife? Will you marry me?"

She looked up at him, surprised. "What? You want to marry me?"

"I want to marry you—again," he said.

Suddenly she pulled away from him, laughing. "I daresay you would not be willing to pay very much for me this time around."

"Pay for you!" he exclaimed in mock exasperation. "I have never stopped paying for you."

"What do you mean?"

"The money you receive every month from your father," he said. "Coulter Manor is doing much better now, but not *that* much better. My solicitor sends it to your father each month for him to send to you."

"Dear Lord! I would never have taken a penny of it had I known!"

"That is exactly why you were not allowed to know," Jason said. "Now, don't start frowning about that; don't waste emotion better spent on something else."

"I am not angry," she said. "I was just thinking. Has it not occurred to you that I may be overpriced?"

"I shall see about that after we are remarried."

"And when will that be?"

"As soon as possible, if I have my way," he said.

"You may always have your way . . . with me," she said teasingly.

Jason laughed, then a serious look came over his face. "There is still one matter I must attend to," he said. "Before we can set a definite date, I must talk to Lord Dysart. I have promised him my services."

Chapter Eight

IT WAS STILL DARK, AN HOUR BEFORE DAWN, when Zandra finished packing the second of her portmanteaus—the same two she had taken to Braley Acres four years earlier—and placed it beside the first in the small entry-way. Not only were the bags the same, but also the gowns and accessories that filled them, for there had been no time to have new gowns made nor even to go on a hurried excursion to the Oxford Street shops.

Jason had returned the day after their reunion and informed her that they were to be guests at a banquet given by the Queen the following week. He and Lord Dysart hoped to talk to her then and make their plans for Jason's trip to France. In the next breath,

Jason proposed that they leave immediately—to be married at Gretna Green in Scotland, near his northern estate. They had decided to leave the very next day. Jason teased her, calling her his eager wench.

He had said that because of the distance they must travel, she would have to be ready before sunrise. It would take most of three long, tiring days, and he had sent a footman on ahead to have their rooms prepared at Melford and to make the necessary arrangements in Gretna Green. Although they were going to the world's capital for runaway marriages, he wanted no impromptu wedding.

Now that everything was in readiness, Emma and Zandra sat waiting near the door.

"I still think I should go with you," Emma said. "No matter that you have been married, you and Jason will spend two nights on the road. Just suppose you cannot find proper accommodations."

Zandra laughed. "If you were along, then there would be three of us inconvenienced instead of merely two."

"It isn't proper that the two of you should travel alone," Emma argued primly. "Now that it is out that you are a divorcée, you are going to have to be very careful about your image. As Jason's wife . . ."

"As Jason's wife, I will no longer be a divorcée," Zandra pointed out. "Besides, you will be moving into Jason's house while we are away and, as he said, bringing order to disorder."

"If his house is as bare as he says, it will take longer than a week to make it livable," Emma contended. "Anyway, I will want your suggestions and help. It will, after all, be your house."

Zandra nodded. The idea of being mistress of the mansion next to Lord and Lady Dysart's still had no reality for her. Her life in the past two days had taken on a dreamlike quality. It was as though she were teetering on the edge of an abyss, terrified of losing her balance and falling in. What if Jason did not come for her? What if the plans they had made, the promises, the love they had shared in the past two days were but a farce, Jason's way of getting revenge on her for leaving him four years ago?

But no, he would not do that, her common sense told her. Jason was not a cruel person; she could not imagine him deliberately hurting anyone. She was reminded again of the terrible hurt she had inflicted upon him by leaving him the morning after their marriage. God willing, she would spend the rest of her life making it up to him.

"You are frowning," Emma said. "Surely you are not having regrets or second thoughts."

"Second and third thoughts," she said, "but

not about marrying Jason. This time I know it is right."

"A good thing, because he has arrived. I hear his carriage in the street."

Jason merely flipped the knocker before he opened the door himself and came in. He was followed by his coachman, who saluted the two women, picked up Zandra's baggage and went out again.

Jason kissed Zandra and then Emma. "We will see you soon," he said, then, looking at his bride, "too soon."

Zandra hugged Emma and then she and Jason were hurrying to the carriage. As they rolled down Curzon Street, she waved to Emma, who was still standing in the doorway. Then she lifted her face to Jason for a kiss more befitting his betrothed than the one with which he had greeted her in the house.

Although Jason had warned her that it would be an arduous journey, Zandra still was not prepared for how tiring it was. The roads, once they had left London and its environs behind, were so deeply rutted that after only a few hours of bumping over them she felt bruised to her very bones. "Does he have to drive so fast?" she asked Jason, nodding toward the coachman.

"If we are to have any time at all at Melford, he does," Jason answered. He adjusted a cushion at her back to make her more comfortable.

At mid-morning they stopped at an inn for refreshment and a change of horses, but then immediately were on their way again. During the afternoon they stopped again for the same purpose.

"It will not be so long now before we stop for the night," Jason told her to boost her flagging spirits. However, at dusk they were traveling through what appeared to be an endless forest with neither clearing nor inn in sight. Zandra's mind was filled at once with every story she had ever heard about highwaymen. "Is it safe to keep going?" she asked. "Do we not run a risk of being robbed or worse?"

"We would be robbed *and* worse if we stopped here," Jason assured her. "There is a village only a few miles ahead where we can put up for the night."

"God be thanked," she murmured.

Jason smiled at her and tightened his arm around her shoulders. He was berating himself for suggesting that they marry in Gretna Green, but he had been so eager to show her his northern estate that, at the time, he had forgotten the difficulty of getting to it. Then too, for them to have remarried in London would have set the gossiping tongues to wagging with such frenzy that they would have had to leave town for a while anyway.

The village finally came into view and the

carriage slowed as it rattled along the narrow street. At the far end of the street stood the Inn of St. George and, without being told, the coachman pulled up at the door. He opened the door for Jason and Zandra. "I will see to the team, sir. What time do we leave in the morning?"

"No later than sunrise," Jason told him and saw Zandra cringe as he said it. "You will feel more like traveling again by morning," he reassured her.

Inside the inn, he bespoke a private parlor and two bedchambers, and Zandra was amazed at the quickness of the service. Jason had a commanding presence and the staff scurried to see to his comfort. *Emma need not have worried about our needing a chaperon,* she thought as she was shown to her room. She was much too fatigued even to give Jason a proper good-night kiss.

The parlor was a very small sitting room with a bedchamber on either side. As Jason went into his, he ordered baths to be sent up for both of them.

"A long soak in a hot bath will get most of the soreness out of you," he told Zandra, "and then a good supper will be in order."

"I am too tired for either," she said, holding to the door frame in weariness.

"Nevertheless, you will have both." He disappeared into his bedchamber.

Zandra fell, fully clothed, across the bed

and was almost asleep when two maidservants entered carrying a large tub, followed by two more with buckets of steaming water. She did not bestir herself until she heard one of the girls say, "Your bath is ready, m'lady."

Three of the girls left the room and the fourth stayed to help her undress and climb into the tub. She sank down into the water, heaving a long sigh as her body relaxed. Never had anything felt so good as the hot water; she could almost feel it taking the stiffness out of her joints. "I may never get out again," she said to the girl.

"Yes, ma'am, you will," the girl said quite seriously. "The water will be stone cold after a while. Do you want me to fetch you more hot water?"

"No, by the time this cools, I'll be ready to sleep," she said.

When Zandra got out of the tub some time later, one of the serving girls returned with a tray containing roast chicken, broiled mushrooms, green beans in cream sauce and piping hot, freshly baked bread. She set the tray on a table beside the bed and turned timidly to Zandra. "The duke ordered supper for you, ma'am."

Zandra had thought she was too tired to eat, but once she tasted the delicious food, she ate with relish. After finishing everything on the tray, she pulled the coverlet of the bed up over herself and rested her head against the bolster. She wondered if Jason would come in to bid her good night, but she was asleep before the thought had fully formed in her mind.

In her dreams, she felt lips grazing lazily across her face then hot kisses on her throat, while through the material of her nightdress she felt the slow stroking . . . caressing. . . . A beautiful dream. . . .

She opened her eyes. The room was dark except for the light from one candle on the stand beside the bed. Jason, in a dressing gown, was lying beside her.

"Jason!" She was startled to see him so near. Modestly, she closed her eyes again and pulled the covers tighter.

"I didn't want to wake you," he said, "and then again, I *did* want to wake you."

She peered at him through half open eyes. His expression was half humorous, half serious. He leaned over her again and his lips found her mouth in an urgent kiss, his hands pressing firmly against her breasts. The world began to whirl giddily as she closed her eyes once more and thrills of desire shot through her like lightning seeking a place to strike.

Then with all the strength she could muster, she pushed at him. "No . . . please," she whispered. "Please not now. I want to wait."

Jason propped himself up on his elbow and looked down at her. He seemed to be looking down from a great height. "But why?" he asked.

"I want everything to be perfect. We've waited so long now to be together. Soon we will be man and wife again and belong truly to each other. Let's wait until then."

A slight frown appeared on his face, then he bent down and gave her a gentle kiss on the forehead. "It will be as you wish," he said, then chuckled, "though my own desire will have to be stilled."

She pulled his head down to hers, kissing him fully on the lips. "Good night, my love."

The second day did not seem so strenuous, though it was no different from the first. She supposed her body had become numb to the jostling and the long hours of sitting. She welcomed the stops for refreshment, but she was glad to be under way again, eager to reach their destination. At one point she remarked to Jason, "It is no wonder eloping couples go to Gretna Green. No parent in his right mind, no matter how irate or disapproving, would ever follow."

The second night was very much like the first, spent in an inn in a small village, but Zandra felt much less fatigued. Before her bath was sent up, Jason asked if she would like to join him in the parlor for supper, which pleased her in spite of her fatigue. They devoured the meal hungrily. When Jason finished, he said, "Tomorrow, my love."

"Tomorrow?"

"Tomorrow we will arrive at Melford, and if you like, you may be the Duchess of Melford by nightfall."

"Duchess?" She looked at him wonderingly. "Duchess!"

"Of course duchess." He seemed surprised at her surprise. "Is not the wife of a duke a duchess?"

"I had not thought of that," she admitted. "I somehow cannot see myself as a duchess."

"I have seen you as nothing else," he smiled, "ever since I came into the dukedom."

She was speechless for so long that he laughed at her. "At least I know you didn't marry me for a title. But when shall it be—our wedding, I mean? Tomorrow?"

"Yes, tomorrow."

"Then we had better retire at once and get all the sleep possible, for there may be little enough tomorrow night."

She reddened and he laughed again. "For one who has been married before, you seem strangely shy."

She nodded, thinking that she probably was more shy this time because she wanted nothing more than to please Jason, to make him as happy as it was possible for mortal man to be.

He took her in his arms then and sought her

mouth with his, seeking, probing, and then suddenly quiescent. He released her. "Go, before I am carried away by your charms. But I give you fair warning, tomorrow night it will be different."

Not quite bold enough to say that she truly hoped so, she bade him good night and went into her small bedchamber, where a serving girl had already prepared her bath. Tonight she spent very little time in the small round tub, and was soon in bed, her thoughts on her wedding day—tomorrow!

Not knowing whether they would go to the duke's estate or the church first, Zandra dressed for her wedding when she awoke the next morning. The serving girl who had been sent to assist her oohed and aahed as she lowered the off-white silk gown brocaded with a rose motif over Zandra's head.

Determined that Jason should not see the gown until they were in the church, Zandra made sure she had on her pelisse when she met him in the small parlor to begin their day on the road. He apparently had had the same idea, for he was wearing a blue dress coat with satin knee breeches and silk hose that showed his muscular, well-shaped legs. They began the last day of their journey and Jason promised her they would arrive soon.

When the carriage arrived at the Kirk o'the Woodlands, Zandra caught her breath and

Jason laughed. "That is why I wanted us to be married in this church," he said. "It is so much like St. John's–in–the–Woods, where we were first married."

He sent the coachman in search of the vicar and helped Zandra to alight from the carriage. By the time they reached the vestibule of the tiny church, the Reverend Mr. MacBain was motioning them to join him in the sanctuary.

Their wedding was simpler and shorter than before, with the minister using the rite of the Scottish Church instead of the English Book of Common Prayer. Zandra looked up at Jason while listening intently to the words the vicar read. Their arms touched lightly and she could almost feel the strength emanating from him. She loved him totally, depended upon him wholly for all the contentment, joy, delight and rapture she would know during the rest of her life.

This is what my whole life has been leading up to, she thought. This is the way I always thought—hoped—my wedding would be.

Though she spoke the vows softly—her eyes on Jason's face as though reading the words of love and honor there—they were repeated in her heart with a resounding echo which she thought must surely have boomed through the small church. And there were other vows she spoke only to herself: I will love you, Jason Braley, as no other has ever loved you

. . . until the end of time. I will cherish you more than life, more than love. All of earth, and even heaven, will envy our devotion.

When the vicar pronounced them man and wife, she knew this time they were joined by love, not merely ceremony, in their minds as well as in the sight of God. This time there were no reservations in Zandra's mind as she made her ardent vows.

Back in the carriage, Jason instructed the coachman to lose no time in getting to Melford Manor, and then, pulling Zandra close to him, he spent most of the ten–minute ride kissing her until she thought she would suffocate. Laughing, he finally released her and said, "I should not distract you the first time you view your new home . . . one of your new homes," he amended.

"Where is it?" she said, leaning to the side to see the surroundings better. There was no house in sight, only a narrow lane lined with trees on both sides.

"This is the avenue to the house," he said.

"Is all this land yours?" she asked, amazed.

"This, and more. The truth is, we have been on my land since we left the kirk."

She was just beginning to get some idea of the extent of his holdings when the "house" came into view.

"House!" she gasped. "It is a palace."

Before her stood a massive stone structure

with three sides built around a courtyard, the fourth side open to allow access to the yard. There were two towers which, Jason told her, had been used as lookout points during the times when England and Scotland were "at odds."

"My uncle told me that sometimes it was difficult to be English and live right on the Scottish border, so our ancestors as a matter of self-preservation often were remarkably adept at hiding their allegiance to whatever monarch was currently displeasing the Scots."

As he helped her from the carriage, she could see servants running into the courtyard and forming a line near the main entrance to the house. Several greeted Jason enthusiastically even before being presented to the new mistress. She could not help but notice the respect and high regard given to Jason and she looked with even more pride at the man she had married.

After accepting the good wishes, bows and curtsies of the servants, she and Jason went inside. After the imposing exterior of the manor, she was expecting an even grander interior, but she was taken through room after room of what might have been a hunting club, full of heavy furniture with little color anywhere. Jason, seeing her consternation, said, "Don't despair. What is needed here is a woman's touch and I propose to let you have a free hand next time we are here. You must remember that my uncle was a bachelor and it has been forty-five or fifty years since the house has had a mistress living in it."

Then he guided her to the master apartment on the second story of the southern wing. There was a comfortable sitting room, a dressing room and a huge bedchamber with the largest bed Zandra had ever seen. Like the rest of the furniture, the bed was of a dark, heavy wood, but the tester was of gold velvet, as were the draperies at the four windows, giving the room a brighter look than any of the others in the house.

"Shall I have some supper sent to us here or would you prefer to eat in the banquet room?" Jason asked, smiling as though he knew the answer but was asking out of politeness.

"Here will be fine," she said.

"I will show you the rest of the house tomorrow," he promised.

"Have I not seen it all?"

"Only about half." He helped her to remove her pelisse, kissing the back of her neck as he did so. "I will send one of the maidservants to help you." As he went to the door, he looked back. "You are so lovely, Zandra. So beautiful." And then he was gone.

The little maid who arrived to help her

seemed awestruck at first by her new mistress; however, Zandra soon put her at ease. She was actually quite talkative, telling Zandra how much the servants—the women, that is—looked forward to having a mistress in the house. "Not one of us be old enough to remember a lady on the premises, ma'am. The men, now, they be another tale. They don't want a lady ordering them around, for they be used to taking orders from a man." She laughed nervously as though afraid she had said too much.

"We'll not be here long enough to give many orders to anybody," Zandra assured her. "We must return to London, but I hope we can come back after the winter is over. I would like to spend the spring here."

"Yes, ma'am." The girl smiled as she helped Zandra into the soft rose-colored peignoir. "You be not afraid?"

It was a moment before Zandra understood what she meant. "No, a little nervous perhaps, but not afraid." It was obvious that the servants did not know she and Jason had been married before.

After brushing the long auburn hair, then standing back to admire Zandra as though she were her own creation, the girl said, "I bid you good night, ma'am."

"Thank you and—oh, what is your name?"

"Megan, ma'am. Megan MacSweeney."

"Good night, Megan, and thank you."

The girl curtsied and left just as Jason returned, followed by a footman bearing a large tray which he placed on a table in the sitting room before discreetly leaving the room.

Zandra looked uncertainly at Jason. "You are making it as much like before as possible. Everything: the church, the supper here in our rooms. Why?"

"Do you object?" Jason asked. "I am not sure why I wanted it this way . . . unless perhaps I wanted to go back and correct the mistakes of the past."

"But the mistakes were mine, not yours."

"I made a few myself." He seemed anxious to drop the subject. "Eat your supper, woman," he commanded. "I grow impatient to exchange the past for the present."

In spite of herself, she colored as she watched him fill her plate with partridge and dried salmon, green goose with French beans, truffles and hot bread. Though the food was delicious, she could not come close to doing it justice. Megan's question kept going through her mind: You be not afraid? She *was* afraid, terrified. Not of Jason nor of making love with him, but afraid that in the four years since their last wedding night he had come to idealize her. What if she did not please him as he had imagined? Would she fulfill his expectations?

"Jason, I . . ." she began, then paused. She laid her fork on her plate.

He reached across the table and grasped her hand. "I know. Let us leave the feasting for later. There are other feasts to be enjoyed."

He had misinterpreted her hesitancy and was helping her up from the table, gently guiding her into the bedchamber. It was too late now to tell him her anxieties, her doubts, for he was slipping the rose peignoir from her shoulders, pressing her against him, his hands caressing her shoulders, her back, and then her breasts.

He picked her up and carried her to the huge bed, removing the nightgown that had been covered by the peignoir. He gave a little gasp and his throat seemed to constrict. "So lovely, so lovely," he said huskily, and he kissed her lips, softly at first, and then with mounting ardor and excitement.

At first she felt limp with embarrassment as his eyes devoured her body, but with his deep, probing kisses, she found her body responding, like a ripple building up into a tidal wave that could not be stilled until it had crashed upon the shore.

He stepped away from the bed, quickly removed his clothing. When he returned to the bed, getting in beside her, Zandra was aware of nothing but his lean, hard body pressed against her as rigid as iron. In that moment, she knew she wanted him as desperately, as achingly as he wanted her.

She felt the heat of his body as he leaned over her, the taste of his mouth as it bore down upon hers, the sensation of his hands as they caressed her breasts—gently for a moment, then more urgently—and then passed on to her secret recesses. She cried out and reached for him, pulling him closer, closer—oh, she could not get him close enough!—as the ecstatic agony mounted in her with lightning rapidity. Jason struggled for restraint, but there was none. He could think only of his frantic, almost desperate craving, and in her eyes he saw the same naked need. Instantly, they came together in a wild embrace, trying to overcome the love-hunger and cold deprivation of the past four years. Wordless, they struggled at the zenith of sensation, trying to go even further, stroking, holding, kissing, possessing . . . and, finally, relinquishing . . . and returning to the moment.

For a long time there was no sound in the room except their breathing. Then he said, "I am sorry, Zandra."

"For what?" she asked, scarcely above a whisper.

"I was not gentle enough, not patient

enough with you. I wanted to give you pleasure as well. But I could not wait . . ."

"Nor could I," she admitted softly, nestling against him, knowing that it would not be very long before desire overcame them both again.

All of her doubts and anxieties were banished forever as she found her body arching to Jason's in yearning desire as he caressed every inch of her, loving her once again, long and sensuously.

Her breasts burned against his chest as though they were aflame, and he covered them, first one and then the other, with his mouth in a futile attempt to extinguish the blaze. Straining to him, she pressed even closer, quivering with anticipation.

More abandoned now, her hands moved over his body, caressing the hard muscles of his arms and back, playing through the coarse hair of his chest, moving down the narrow hips to the shaft of his manhood. There was not an inch of his body that she did not yearn for.

He groaned with pleasure at her touch and then his seeking mouth explored her body with fervid tenderness, finding all her hidden sweetness. They were together again in the timeless rhythm of love, building slowly, gradually, accelerating to a crescendo and, again, release.

Much later, before Jason blew out the three candles in the candelabrum beside the bed, Zandra remembered the words of the marriage ceremony, ". . . with my body I thee worship," and she understood now the full meaning of those words.

Chapter Nine

"IN MY ENTIRE LIFE I NEVER HEARD OF ANYONE sitting down to supper at three o'clock in the afternoon," Zandra complained.

"The reason, I think, is that there are so many courses that it will take well into the night to serve them all," Jason said.

"It is small wonder then that the Queen is as big as a behemoth," Zandra retorted.

They were in the master bedchamber of the Mount Street house in London dressing for the Queen's banquet. Only yesterday they had returned from what they now called their northern estate. She had not wanted to leave, so happy had she been during the three nights they had spent there. Her life had changed so much—not only her life but her whole way of looking at things, her attitude, her dreams—in so short a time. "If only we could stay a little

159

longer," she had said to Jason an hour before their departure. "I know it is silly of me, but I am afraid we will not be so happy anywhere else."

Jason laughed at her. "That is a strange form of superstition. As long as we are together, we can be happy anywhere."

She nodded. "But may we come back to finish our honeymoon? Perhaps spend the spring here?"

"Of course. But our honeymoon will never be finished." And he had kissed her passionately.

The trip back to London had not seemed as long or as tiring as the one to Melford. They shared a bedchamber, and though neither of them got much sleep, they found comfort enough lying with limbs entangled, bodies pressed together.

Now Zandra looked at her clothes, hastily unpacked the day before. "Nothing I have will do," she told her husband. "If only there had been time for me to have some gowns made. The Queen is apt to mistake me for one of the serving girls."

"No chance of that, my sweet. Not even if you dressed in livery and carried a tray. Here, let me look." He peered into the wardrobe and finally took out a gown of white sarsenet. "This will do quite well."

"But Jason, that is for warmer weather. This is almost the dead of winter."

"No matter." He took out a white fringed shawl. "This will keep off the drafts of the Banqueting House. You are a bride and this attire looks bridal."

"If you don't care that I'm somewhat out of fashion, then I shan't either."

"Good God, woman! I shall be the envy of every man present! Out of fashion, indeed!" He kissed her soundly, then went down to order the carriage brought around.

The Banqueting House was awesome, Zandra thought upon her first glimpse of it. It had served as a sort of auxiliary building to Whitehall Palace, which had burned to the ground some years before. Saved from the disastrous fire, the Banqueting House was a long room, ostentatiously appointed.

Zandra started as the Keeper of the Door announced their arrival in tones that could have been heard on the other side of the Thames. "The Duke and Duchess of Melford."

A shiver went through her at hearing her title for the first time. She looked up at her duke and smiled radiantly, and he gave her just the tiniest wink, perceptible only to her.

At the upper end of the long room sat an elevated throne. Below the dais tables extended for the lords and ladies of the court and at the far end of the elongated hall were two orchestras that would play in turn during the afternoon and evening. Along the walls, wax tapers already burned in silver sconces even though it was broad daylight outside. The Life Guards stood, strategically placed near the dais, splendidly outfitted, with white feathers that drooped over the broad brims of their hats, scarlet coats richly trimmed in gold lace and cascades of ruffles. Their weapons were short carbines, pistols and swords.

Jason, amused at her wonderstruck expression, told her to look at the ceiling. She could hardly believe what she saw. King James I was portrayed on his way to heaven, wafted skyward by rosy cherubs who looked wholly unequal to the task.

"The painting is a reminder that James I held his scepter and orb by divine right," Jason said, "and therefore could do no wrong."

She gave him a disbelieving look and he laughed. "Oh—over there, Lord and Lady Dysart have arrived. We are to sit with them, I believe." He steered her through several groups of beautifully dressed peers and their ladies to the side of the hall where Lord and Lady Dysart were just disengaging themselves from a smaller group.

"There you are, Jason," Lord Dysart said. "I was wondering if you had arrived. Good afternoon, Your Grace." He bowed to Zandra.

"Good afternoon, your lordship, your ladyship," Zandra said, inclining her head to both.

It was the first time she had seen them since the night of their party for Jason, and though she expected Lord Dysart to be polite, she had no idea what to expect from the woman who, as her hostess, had all but ignored her.

Lady Dysart bowed slightly and murmured, "Good afternoon." Obviously, she could not completely ignore a duchess, though it was apparent that she wanted to.

Lord Dysart tried to ease the tension. "We have been here for a good half hour and I am getting tired of standing," he remarked jovially. "I wish the Queen would make her entrance so we could all sit down."

Even as he spoke a hush fell upon the room as a trumpeter entered at the far end to herald the arrival of the monarch. Zandra craned her neck to get her first look at Queen Anne.

The Queen limped into the room, a huge, homely woman. She was fat, prematurely aged and crippled with gout. Her reddish-brown hair was streaked with gray, hanging limply to her shoulders, and atop her head sat a jeweled coronet with a cross at the front. She wore a gold brocaded gown with white mink panels down the front and the full sleeves, and at her waist a wide gold belt decorated with pearls.

In spite of the grandeur of her dress, what most impressed Zandra was the Queen's ashen face, her expression of acute pain.

"Brandy-faced Nan is living up to her

name," Lady Dysart said to her husband in a whisper loud enough to be heard by all standing in the vicinity. "She can scarcely walk to the throne."

"The woman is sick, not drunk," Zandra said, outraged. "Can you not tell by her face that she is really quite ill?"

"Yes, I heard this undertaking was quite an effort for her," Lord Dysart said quickly. "It will probably be her last social occasion." He gave Jason a meaningful look. "I understand we will have little chance of getting the Queen's ear today. When I inquired about an audience, I was told there would be no talk of a political nature. Her Majesty is not well and will not discuss anything of moment."

"I am disappointed," Jason said. "I wanted to hear the Queen's express wishes concerning the task we are undertaking."

The Queen, at that moment, was with great difficulty preparing to sit down upon the throne. She grasped the arms, then slowly lowered herself into the seat.

"Dear Lord, she may not last through the meal," Lady Dysart said, obviously having changed her mind about the state of the Queen's sobriety.

The Queen motioned toward the guests in the hall and the approximately two hundred people found their seats at the long tables while one of the orchestras struck up an old English air.

Jason and Zandra sat at the end of one table with Lord and Lady Dysart at Jason's right. Jason deliberately had suggested that Lord Dysart sit beside him, not only to separate the two women as far as possible but also to allow him to talk further with his lordship about the details of his proposed trip to France.

Liveried footmen began serving the enormous meal. There was beef, mutton, duck, chicken, rabbit, turkey pie, shrimp pie, venison pasties, salmon pie fringed with gold, almonds, oranges, raisins, sweet fruits preserved and dried, puddings of every description, and custard florentine. At least two dozen different kinds of wine were served and a half dozen wine goblets were set before each guest. In horror and amazement, Zandra saw the man on her left empty a goblet of rich red wine, turn slightly in his chair and throw the goblet against the wall.

She jumped and leaned toward Jason for protection from the maniac, fully expecting one of the Life Guards to eject the man bodily from the hall. However, no one so much as raised an eyebrow in surprise, and it was only a matter of moments before a second and third goblet were heard to smash in the other end of the hall.

"Am I in Bedlam?" Zandra whispered to Jason. "What *is* happening here?"

Jason laughed. "I am not sure how the

custom started, but I am told the upper class likes the sound of breaking glass."

"You mean one has to break a perfectly good goblet to prove he is of the upper class?"

"No proof is necessary here," Jason told her. "You can be sure every one of the Queen's guests is indeed of the upper class."

Zandra said nothing but glanced pointedly at Lady Dysart.

A footman leaned over and whispered something to Jason, who arose from the table immediately. "Come, we are to be presented to the Queen by Viscount Bolingbroke," he said, and pulled out Zandra's chair to help her up.

Her stomach fluttery, her hand trembling slightly as she placed it in Jason's, she said lightly, "First I am going to have to be presented to Viscount Bolingbroke."

"As am I," said Jason, looking to Lord Dysart to do the honors.

The viscount was sitting near the end of a table almost directly below the dais. Zandra had heard the Queen's secretary of state described as brilliant and unstable, and looking into his shrewd little eyes as she and Jason were introduced, she could well imagine that he was both. But Henry St. John, the Viscount Bolingbroke, paid scant heed to Zandra and studied Jason instead as though he were sizing up new blood he had thoughts of buying. Apparently Jason passed the test, for Bolingbroke shook his hand and then edged the couple toward the dais.

"Your Majesty, may I present to you the Duke and Duchess of Melford."

There was a moment of silence that threatened to become awkward: then the Queen said in a low, strained voice, "I do not believe I have seen you before."

"No, Your Majesty," Jason said. "I am comparatively new to London . . ." He was unsure how to go on. He knew this was neither the time nor the place to broach what was really on his mind. "I wonder, Your Majesty, if I might have a word with you after the banquet?"

The Queen's eyes darted questioningly to Bolingbroke. "The duke is the one of whom I spoke to you," he prompted. "He has agreed to go to St. Germain for us."

The Queen nodded slowly and looked back at Jason. "Perhaps later," she said, dismissing them both by concentrating upon the plate of food balanced precariously on her lap.

Zandra could feel little more than pity for the woman. Close up, it was possible to see better what the ravages of illness had done to her, as well as—some would have it— imbibing too frequently. It seemed impossible to Zandra that this monarch ever could have had the stamina to veto an act of Parliament or preside over the Cabinet. Anne was only in her forty-eighth year, yet there was truly the look of death about her.

Once they resumed eating, Zandra could only catch an occasional word of the conversation that ensued between Jason and Lord Dysart. Politics, she thought, always politics. She wished fervently that Lord Dysart had not chosen Jason to be his messenger to the Pretender. The thought of being separated from Jason for even a day overwhelmed her, and it might take weeks to make the trip to France. She knew he couldn't take her with him. She only hoped that he would be as anxious to return to her as she would be to have him back.

Zandra listened with scant interest to the conversation around her. Then suddenly she had a strange feeling that eyes were upon her, staring mercilessly. She looked down the table at the faces one by one, all of them unfamiliar, until at last she started in recognition. Near the end of the table, Gower slouched and stared at her moodily. Then he shifted his gaze to Jason, looking at his rival with murder in his eye.

Chapter Ten

EVEN AS ZANDRA CRINGED UNDER GOWER'S malignant stare, a sudden, eerie hush fell over the enormous hall. The orchestra stopped, all conversation ceased, and even the sounds of cutlery on plates and tinkling crystal were stilled. All eyes turned to the throne to see if the Queen had ordered the silence, but Anne was no longer on the dais. She was being helped from the room, too ill to remain through supper.

"She has been nipping along more than usual," the man beside Zandra said in a loud whisper.

"The Queen is ill, quite ill," Zandra retorted angrily.

"And I know what made her ill," the man

said, this time not bothering to lower his voice.

Before she could reply, the Viscount Bolingbroke stepped up on the dais and announced that due to a sudden indisposition the Queen had found it necessary to retire, but that she had requested that the banquet not be interrupted. He left the dais and then walked down the long hall to Lord Dysart. "Her Majesty has requested that you and I and the Duke of Melford join her in an anteroom for a few minutes before she is taken back to St. James Palace."

The two men hastily excused themselves and followed the viscount. The Queen was already outside, being helped into her coach, and she gestured for the three men to get in. She lost no time with amenities but got right to the point.

"I have been asked, time and again, to put a price on my brother James's head," she said, "and that I cannot and *will* not do. Not as long as there is a chance that he might be dissuaded from the disastrous route he appears to have taken." She looked at Jason. "I understand you think you can effect a reconciliation between James and Protestant England."

"No, Your Majesty," Jason said immediately. "I have said only that I am willing to try. I most assuredly cannot promise success where so many others have failed; I would be foolhardy even to suggest such a thing."

Anne stared at him, her eyes dulled by pain. "Nevertheless, I would like for you to try. When will you go to France?"

Jason looked uncertainly at Lord Dysart and Viscount Bolingbroke. "How soon could you make yourself ready?" the viscount asked.

Not for the first time, Jason was sorry he had allowed himself to be brought into partisan matters involving the crown. Although he saw wisdom in restoring James to the throne, his main consideration at the moment was Zandra. He was loath to leave her so soon after their marriage, but, he supposed, the sooner he left, the sooner he could return.

"I can be ready to leave two days hence."

The Queen nodded. "I would like to see this one last attempt made. I would like for my half brother to come back, but only if he will give up his Catholicism." She sighed deeply. "I do not want to be responsible for blood running in the streets."

Although the banquet should have lasted until well into the night, the guests were preparing to leave shortly after eight o'clock. The Queen's departure had dampened the lively atmosphere of celebration even more than her arrival.

Waiting for their carriages to be brought around, Zandra and Jason stood with Lord and Lady Dysart. "Since it is yet early, could you and . . . and Zandra come in for a visit when we get home?" Dysart suggested. "There are things that must be discussed, Jason."

Jason accepted the invitation. Too late, he saw Zandra's frown.

They were barely seated in the Dysarts' salon before Lord Dysart began. "I talked with Bolingbroke again just before we left the hall. He will make the necessary arrangements for your channel crossing and have a carriage waiting on the other side to take you to the Pretender."

Zandra suddenly felt as ill as the Queen had looked. "When are you to leave?" she asked Jason.

"Not for two days yet," he said in a cheerful tone. He had not wanted her to find out in this way, but now that she knew he didn't want to burden her with his own misgivings.

"How long will you be gone?" was her next question.

"I—I am not sure." Jason looked at Lord Dysart.

"I imagine that will depend upon James's mood," Lord Dysart said. "If he seems on the brink of converting, then I suggest you stay as long as necessary to persuade him. On the other hand, if he seems immovable, then you may as well come back at once."

"Then there's no way of knowing," Zandra said miserably.

Lord Dysart gave her a kindly look. "I realize you are newly married . . ." He broke off and coughed as though unsure whether he had made a *faux pas,* then continued, "I realize that this is a bad time for a separation, but Monrovia and I will try to see that you do not have too much free time in which to miss Jason, won't we, my dear?"

"Indeed," Lady Dysart said unenthusiastically.

"But this is winter and the channel will be rough," Zandra said, the thought just occurring to her. The more she thought about Jason's mission to France, the more wretched she became. "Please, could not the journey wait until spring?"

"Absolutely not," Lord Dysart said at once. "You saw the Queen tonight. It is hardly likely that she will last through the winter, let alone until spring. No, if James is to come back, it must be as soon as possible. How much better it would have been if he had come back years ago—as his sister's loyal subject."

As the footman entered with a tray bearing a decanter of brandy, Jason stood up. "I must beg you to excuse us now. It is later than I thought and I must begin preparations for my journey at once." He neglected to mention that the first of his "preparations" was to get Zandra home and make love to her. Seeing the love and concern on her face during the discussion had filled him with tenderness and then desire. All he wanted at this minute was to be alone with her, to undress her and revel in her loveliness, to feel her warm softness assuaging his pulsating need. He could not bear to share her with any other people right now. He must have her all to himself, to feast his eyes, and then his body. They quickly took their leave.

"Well, I must say they were in a dreadful hurry to rid themselves of our company," Lady Dysart remarked archly after they left. "Did we insult them in any way? I certainly made a great effort not to."

Lord Dysart laughed. "No, they were not insulted. Think, Rovie. Can you not remember how it was when we were first married?"

She gave him her first genuine smile of the evening. "Almost, Evander. Almost."

Chapter Eleven

GOWER SAT ALONE IN HIS ROOMS, GOING OVER
and over in his mind the grim finale to the
Queen's banquet. He had learned that she
had been taken to Windsor Castle the following day and was not expected to see London
ever again. Something was going to happen
very soon—and Gower was determined to
have a major role. But Melford was the one
chosen to go to France. That name turned his
thoughts in another direction.

It was not to be endured. It simply was *not*
to be endured! Jason Braley, the Duke of
Melford, had upset—no, more than upset—
had *ruined* Gower's life. Only a fortnight ago
he had been in love with a beautiful woman,
the most desirable woman he had ever seen,

and had planned to marry her. He could somehow have borne the news that she was divorced. After all, had he not overcome that obstacle by asking her to become his mistress? Surely no right-thinking woman could have expected an offer of marriage from a peer of the realm once it was known that she was divorced. Damn Jason Braley! Zandra had shown every sign of returning his love and then Braley had come back into her life, wreaking havoc with Gower's feelings as well as his future.

Surely there must be some way to break up that miserable marriage. Zandra had left Braley once; was it not possible that she could leave him again? Gower did not for a minute believe that strange excuse of hers that she had left only because it had been an arranged marriage. Were not all marriages arranged, at least for women? No, there had to be another reason, something else that had sent her fleeing from the duke's bed and board. If only he could talk to her alone for a few minutes, he was sure he could find out . . . and once he knew, he was even surer that he could talk her into leaving Braley again.

And what was worse about Melford, the man was not content with stealing Gower's ladylove, he had also stolen—or was about to—the glory that should be Gower's. *He* should be the one to go to St. Germain, persuade the Pretender to become a Protestant, and come back to England triumphant. *He* should be the one to have the everlasting thanks of his grateful country for keeping a Stuart on the throne.

By God, something had to be done, and right now. He could not delay another minute. He must come up with a way to tarnish Braley's good image and break up his marriage. Then he could take the credit for bringing James back, and take Zandra as his mistress. A plan began to form in his mind.

It was highly unlikely that Braley could, in the space of a few days, talk the devout James into renouncing Catholicism, but he could, most likely, get him into a pensive mood. And once James had had plenty of time to think of the advantages of turning Protestant, then Gower could go to France and with little or no difficulty finish the job. He and James would then come back together, just as he had imagined so many times.

As for the rest of the plan concerning Zandra, he already had devised a scheme he was sure would work. The town tongue-waggers would soon hear that Zandra's second marriage to Braley had lasted scarcely longer than her first.

"Emma, I am counting upon you to keep Zandra from fretting too much while I am gone," Jason said, looking affectionately at his aunt-in-law. The three of them were in the dining parlor, just finishing supper.

"I shall certainly do my utmost," Emma said cheerfully, knowing that in this instance she really had her job cut out for her. Already Zandra had a stricken look, like one bereaved. "But as you well know, Jason, your wife is inclined to be a bit headstrong. If she makes up her mind that she wants to mope about and be miserable every minute you're gone, then she'll do it, come famine, flood or the final trump of judgment."

Jason laughed and even Zandra smiled. "You're right," he said, rising. "Now, if you ladies will excuse me, I had better go supervise Jeremiah as he packs."

"I'll pack for you, Jason," Zandra said, getting up immediately and following him from the dining parlor. "You'll not need Jeremiah."

In the master bedchamber, Jason took his clothes from the huge oak wardrobe and Zandra placed them in the large portmanteau. "Please don't look so grim," he told her. "It will only be for a day or two, four or five at the very most."

She gave him a forced smile and finished her task as he sat on the edge of the bed watching her with a strange hunger in his eyes. "Come here," he said when she had put the last neckcloth into the bag.

She came and stood before him like a little girl, hands clasped behind her back.

"You look as though you are about to be punished," he said.

"I am," she replied. "You're going away."

"Zandra, Zandra, what am I to do with you?" He caught her around the waist and pulled her to him.

Slowly, he slipped her gown off her shoulders, down her body and over her rounded hips to a little heap on the floor. She stepped out of it and then out of her petticoats and, clad only in her chemise, lay down on the bed while he hurriedly removed his clothing. He freed her from the chemise with gentle hands and then, for a minute or two, refrained from touching her while his eyes devoured her.

Already aching for his touch, she strained toward him. He ran his hand down the curves of her body as though exploring them for the first time, as though he had not already memorized every inch of her. He kissed the smooth neck and felt the throbbing pulse of her throat, his own body responding eagerly and with urgency to her caresses. His lips left her throat and sought her breasts, causing her to writhe in anticipation.

With maddening slowness he began to pull the pins out of her hair until the auburn tresses cascaded across the pillow. Then, and only then, did his lips cover hers again in deep, ravenous kisses, moving maddeningly down her body, finally reaching the core of her desire.

Waves of pleasure made her whole body tingle as he brought her nearer and nearer to the edge of ecstasy, hesitating just as she reached the brink, causing her to cry out and try to pull him to her straining body.

Still he hesitated, teasing her, tormenting her with his tongue that moved over her body, scalding her everywhere it touched. His arms wound around her tightly, holding her so closely against him that she could feel the pounding of her heart, the weight of his pulsating manhood. She ran her hands through his hair, twisting the dark strands around her fingers and she nuzzled his ear.

His own desire, curbed to give her pleasure, had mounted to an unbearable peak. It could not be stilled much longer. . . .

When he lifted her hips to his, she welded herself to him, her body ablaze with the fever of love. Finally, both overcome by their urgent need for each other, they soared to new heights of delight, attaining at last that supreme moment of ecstasy and oneness.

For several minutes they lay exhausted in each other's arms, the shuddering torrents of the aftermath of love gradually quieting. Only then did Jason realize she was crying.

"Zandra," he said softly, "what is it, love?"

For a long while she said nothing, and just when he was beginning to think she would not answer, she said, "I'm afraid."

"Afraid of what?" He did not think there was anything under the sun that could frighten her, from fear of an uncertain future to gossiping dowagers.

Instead of answering his question, she raised her head, looked at him through tear-dimmed eyes and pleaded, "Oh, Jason, please don't go. *Please!*"

"But I must, my sweet. You know that."

"No, you *mustn't*." She clutched at him as though trying to restrain him right then. "You can't! Please, Jason, I have the worst feeling about this journey, the most vivid foreboding—"

"You are not superstitious," he interrupted. "You are much too intelligent to be thinking like that."

"It is not superstition," she insisted. "Somewhere deep inside me I *know* that if you leave me now, something terrible is going to happen." She lowered her voice to a whisper. "We may never see each other again."

"Zandra." He held her even closer. "If only there were some way I could make you see that your worrying is all for naught. You'll not only see me again, you'll probably see me much sooner than you expect, long before you and Emma have done all the things you plan to do while I am gone."

She had no answer for him. There was no way she could convey to him the terror she felt in her heart. Never before had she had such a strong feeling, a premonition so powerful, of impending disaster.

Chapter Twelve

JASON, HIS FACE PRESSED AGAINST THE THICK glass of the square porthole, stared out at the gray, raging water. Were the weather not so abominably cold, with snow-laden clouds hovering just above the channel, he would swear that the water was boiling, for that was how it appeared.

His stomach lurched and he sat down on the long bench again. Though not given to seasickness, he felt a bit queasy now. The water was unusually rough and seemed even rougher because of the smallness of the boat.

The postboat was an added precaution. Though his mission was well known, it would be assumed either that the Queen would send him in a royal craft, or else that he would use one of the small commercial ships that made regular crossings. Anyone who might want to sabotage the trip would not look for him here.

In a way, Jason was glad the crossing was rough. At least it prevented the passengers from engaging in conversation, and the last thing he wanted to do right now was talk. He could think only of Zandra, of the way she had looked and spoken when he had left early that morning.

Once again she had implored him not to go, and again he had found that his reassurances were in vain. Finally, when she said good-bye, she had clung to him as though she honestly believed it to be their final parting. He could not understand why she was so distraught over a simple journey to France, she who was usually so sensible about things. Could it be more than a premonition? Did she actually know something about the mission that he did not? Of course not, he chided himself instantly. If she had, she would have told him. No, her strange behavior *had* to spring from the fact that they were so recently married and she did not want to be separated from him for even a few hours.

He felt the same way, but because of her fears, he had not told her how much he himself dreaded the separation. He would count every hour, every minute until he could be back with her again, holding her in his arms, making love to her . . .

It was growing dark now and, if possible, the sea was even rougher than before. It almost made him ill to think that the trip was just beginning and that after landing in Calais, he still would have to make the journey to St. Germain. At least he would have a private carriage, arranged by Lord Dysart, to take him to the Pretender.

It was totally dark when the small boat docked at Calais. Jason went down the slightly rocking gangway to the wharf, stopped and looked around. There was not much activity visible in the torchlight, so he walked to the end of the wharf.

"Monsieur le duc?" questioned a voice at his elbow, causing him to start.

"Oui," he said, turning to face a very short, bearded man in a greatcoat with the hood pulled up. In the light of the flickering torches it was impossible to see his features, other than a large protruding nose.

"Your full name?" The man switched to English.

"Jason Braley, the Duke of Melford."

"And you are here to . . ." The man stopped, waiting for Jason to supply the reason.

"To talk with the Pretender to the English throne, James Stuart."

The man nodded, satisfied. "Come with me." He took Jason's portmanteau from him and started walking hurriedly down the street.

"Wait," Jason said. "I was told there was to be a carriage here to meet me. Where is it?"

The man turned. "You are not to go to St. Germain. I am taking you to *Les Trois Lunes*, where you will pass the night. Tomorrow the *Chevalier de St. George* will arrive and you will talk here in Calais."

"Why is James coming here?" Jason asked, immediately suspicious at this change of plan.

"He was traveling in Belgium when he received word that he was to have a visitor. He deemed it better to meet you here than for you both to waste time going to St. Germain."

The man seemed to speak truthfully. Jason nodded and followed the man down the street.

The noise in his dream seemed to be of a tumultuous sea and a small ship with every timber creaking. Then he was suddenly awake and realized that the noise was at his door. He was not sure of the hour, for the light filtering through the half-open shutters was a gloomy gray. He sat up in bed, orienting himself.

The knocking continued, with a voice added to it. *"Monsieur le duc! Monsieur le duc!"*

He recognized the voice as that of his guide of last night. Looking at the door, he discovered to his dismay that in his fatigue he had forgotten to throw the bolt. *"Entrez,"* he called, getting out of bed and putting on a long woolen robe.

The man stuck his head around the door and then came in, closing the door firmly behind him. *"Le Chevalier* awaits you below in a parlor," he said.

"He is *here*?" Jason asked, surprised, then, "What is the hour?"

"Ten."

"I am sorry," Jason said. "I overslept. I should have found out last night what time we were to meet today."

"I did not know last night," the man said without further explanation. "Come, I will take you now."

"May I dress first?" He wondered if this ridiculous little man really thought he would go to meet the man who might be the future King of England attired in a nightshirt and with a day's growth of beard.

The man nodded, gave a put-upon sigh, and sat down. Jason proceeded to make himself presentable, giving the man surreptitious looks as he did so. Today he could see more than the oversized nose. Jason's escort was middle-aged, balding and leaning toward obesity. The black beard was almost too severe a contrast to the high forehead and receding hairline.

"May I know your name?" Jason asked as he dressed.

"It is not necessary that you do."

Jason paused and looked at him suspiciously. "Is there any reason why I should not know your name?"

"No, but neither is there any reason why you should."

Apparently that was that! Jason finished tying his neckcloth, turned to his unknown guide and said, "I am ready."

"There will be food in the parlor," the man said. *"Le Chevalier* is eating breakfast now."

"I am not hungry," Jason said. "I can wait." He reached into his bag and retrieved the document that James was supposed to sign if he agreed to the terms of his return to England.

The two men went downstairs and then down a long hallway, and at a door at the end of the hall Jason's companion knocked, calling softly, "Marceau, *c'est moi et monsieur le duc.*" Then he went quickly back down the hall, leaving Jason alone.

The door was opened by a tall, gray-haired man who stepped outside, looked Jason over carefully, then pushed the door open again and indicated that Jason was to go in. "He awaits," was all he said, then he, too, went down the long hallway.

Jason entered the room, a small parlor elaborately decorated with purple velvet portieres, which had not been drawn, a purple rug and furniture upholstered in purple velvet. Gold sconces on the wall held tall candles. The room obviously was the innkeeper's idea of a place to entertain royalty, Jason thought.

Only on a second glance around the room did he spot the royalty that was being entertained. James Francis Edward Stuart was all but lost in a large purple chair almost as wide as it was tall. He neither moved nor spoke for a minute or two and Jason stood quietly until he was addressed.

Without appearing to do so, he studied the Pretender with every bit as much curiosity as he himself was being examined. There was some small resemblance to a portrait Jason had seen of Charles II. James had the same dark, intense eyes and dark hair that hung lankly about his face. In the huge chair, he appeared small and frail, sickly-looking.

Finally he spoke. "You are the Duke of Melford, sent by the Viscount Bolingbroke?"

"I am, sir."

James arose from the chair as slowly as though he were an invalid. "For what purpose?" he asked.

"I believe you know, sir. Others have come before me."

James gave a wan smile and moved to a table in the corner that was laden with covered dishes. "Will you eat?" he asked.

"Thank you, no. I am here to talk, sir."

"As you like." James sat down at the table,

uncovered one of the dishes and pulled off a quarter of a loaf of freshly baked bread. "Well, sit, man. Don't hover over me like a servant."

"Thank you, sir." Jason sat across the table from the man who would be king.

"Are you to be my escort back to England?" James asked suddenly.

Trying not to look surprised, Jason said, "I would like to be, sir, if you are ready to return."

"I have been ready for many a long year. It is not I who will not listen to reason, it is some of those hardheaded, crackbrained . . ." He broke off, adding, "And I suppose you are one of them."

"I hope that I shall always be able to see both sides of an issue, my lord."

"You are a Protestant, of course."

"Church of England," Jason said.

"I thought as much." James nodded while chewing thoughtfully on the bread. "And can you see both sides of *this* issue then?"

"I can see that, if you would be King of England, you must be prepared to protect, preserve and defend the Church of England."

"Never!" With a petulant motion, James threw the bread in his hand across the room. "There is only one true church on this earth, the Holy Catholic Church. I *will* be King of England, and I will bring the Mother Church back to England. God has chosen me to reestablish His Church in a country that has fallen on ways of sin and shame. *I* will bring my country back to the Church and God."

Jason knew already that his mission had failed, failed before it had begun. James was as fanatic about his religion as his followers were about him. Jason looked into the pale face of the sickly man, and instead of an inspiring leader he saw a devout man, a man whose religion would always come first. James possessed none of the qualities that would make him a good leader, except where his church was concerned.

"You understand the reasons, I am sure, why you must renounce the Roman Church if you are to reign," Jason said. "There would be insurrection the moment you set foot on English soil if it was thought that you were returning to persecute the Protestants and do away with the Church of England."

James shrugged. "How can you say there would be insurrection? Only God knows what will happen in the future. We are vouchsafed no such clairvoyance."

"True, sir," Jason said. He reached into his coat and brought out the document he had hoped to return with James's signature. "I have here a draft declaration in which you are to renounce the Roman Catholic Church. If I return this paper with your signature, you will be welcomed back to England by all. I gather, however, that you wish me to return the document without your signature."

To his surprise, James held out his hand for the paper. "I will look at it," he said. "You may go now, as we have nothing more to say to each other."

Jason was uncertain whether he meant for him merely to leave the room or to go back to England. "Do you wish to talk again?" he asked.

James shrugged again. That was his only answer.

Jason left the room and went to the public dining room, where he ordered a huge breakfast. After he finished eating he went outside to stretch his legs. The day was still bleak and cheerless and an occasional snowflake gave indication of snowfall to come. Jason viewed the clouds with alarm, knowing that if the weather became too fierce, no ships or boats would cross the channel. If only Zandra were with him he could consider the journey a pleasure outing and enjoy it to the fullest now that he had done the business for which he had come.

And a bad business it was, too, he thought as he walked about the streets of Calais. He did not relish the thought of having to tell Lord Dysart and Bolingbroke that not only had he failed, but also that he himself was not too sorry that he had. James seemed to be the embodiment of all of the Stuart weaknesses and none of the Stuart charm. He would make, at best, a weak, inadequate and unsound ruler. At worst, he could tear England apart philosophically, in religion, in relations with all other countries but France, and, quite literally, if the much-feared, often-spoken-of insurrection came to pass. No matter how bad the Electress of Hanover and her son were, they could do no worse than that.

Suddenly a bright copper-colored bonnet in the window of a millinery shop attracted his attention. It would be stunning on Zandra, the copper blending beautifully with her near-red hair. He went in and purchased the bonnet, missing her sorely.

He had gone only a little way farther when he found himself looking in the window of a jeweler's shop at a set of emerald earrings and a matching necklace. He almost chuckled out loud as he thought how magnificent *they* would look on Zandra, for the stones were the same shade as her eyes. He made his second purchase and then returned to *Les Trois Lunes*.

He waited in the inn until dusk with no word from anyone, but as he was leaving the hostelry he was stopped at the door by the man called Marceau who bowed and said, "Your Grace, *Le Chevalier* will see you tomorrow."

His disappointment showing plainly on his face, Jason asked, "At what hour?"

"I will let you know tomorrow."

"I thought our discussion was over," he said, more than a little disgruntled at having to postpone his departure.

"I think not." With that Marceau went to the back of the building where, apparently, the Pretender had taken rooms.

After ordering supper to be sent up, Jason returned to his room. He ate with only half an appetite and retired early, thinking the best way to pass the time quickly was to sleep. Sleep eluded him, though, and he spent a long, restless night wishing for Zandra. It was impossible to lie in bed without longing for her warm softness beside him, without aching to hold her. Just thinking about her made his body pulsate with desire. Oh, to be back home with her! He would promise her then that they would never be apart again. Her forebodings had been unfounded, as she would realize, but his homesickness for her was as great as any physical illness. Never would he allow them to be separated from one another again.

With that thought, he fell into a troubled sleep.

He awoke early, dressed, and went down to the public room for breakfast. He looked about the building, but there was no sign of

Marceau or "the unknown." The morning passed slowly and the afternoon dragged by but still there was no summons. Finally, impatient to have it over, Jason went to the proprietor and requested that he be taken to James Stuart.

The man, whose head seemed too large for his body, gave Jason a strange look and told him there was no one there by that name.

"Le Chevalier de St. George," Jason said in disgust.

The proprietor threw up his hands and told Jason in rapid French that, to his knowledge, there were no knights of St. George or of any other saint in his hostelry.

Even more disgusted, Jason went back to his room.

Another night passed in much the same way as the preceding one. Finally on the following morning, as Jason sat in the public room, Marceau appeared, looking tired and drawn, and whispered to Jason, *"Le Chevalier* is ready to sign the document."

Astonished, Jason followed the man back to the same parlor in which he had talked to James two days before. Was it possible?

James was sitting in the same huge chair, Bolingbroke's draft document in his hand. Without so much as a "good morning" he said to Jason, "I will sign."

"You are willing to renounce Rome, give up

the Catholic Church for good and all, accept Protestantism and vow to defend the Church of England?" Jason asked perfunctorily.

"Of course not!" James snapped. "What would give you that imbecilic idea?"

"That's what it means if you sign that paper."

"I am prepared to write a paper of my own," he said. "I will promise the Protestants reasonable security."

"Reasonable security!" Jason exploded. "That is totally impossible!"

"I cannot give up my religion." For a moment the misery in the man's eyes caused Jason to pity him.

"I can understand that," Jason told him, "and I can even admire you for it. But a promise of reasonable security—whatever that may be—will not satisfy the Protestants of England, nor will a Catholic king be permitted to reign. If that is all you can offer, then I must bid you farewell and return with your decision."

Jason waited a moment, but James did not speak. Finally, Jason said, "I bid you good day, my lord." When he reached the door, he turned and added, "And I wish you well."

Chapter Thirteen

THE DAY OF JASON'S DEPARTURE AND THE next morning, Zandra moped about the house like an invalid. Emma watched silently for a while, but even she had been unprepared for the absolute misery in Zandra's eyes. She finally persuaded her niece to join her for tea late that morning.

"I really am neither hungry nor thirsty, Emma," Zandra protested.

"I doubt if Jason will be pleased to return from France and find you half starved," Emma said curtly. She poured a cup of tea for her niece and put a pastry on the saucer beside the cup. "Now eat. I do not want an invalid on my hands."

She watched as Zandra forced herself to go through the motions of eating and drinking. If she goes on like this, the older woman thought, *I* shall be as eager for Jason's return as she. Emma said, "Don't you think you've carried on like this long enough?"

Looking up from her saucer, Zandra said, "What do you mean?"

"I mean it is normal for newlyweds who are separated to *miss* each other, but you are acting as though Jason has gone forever, as though he were dead." The instant she said it, Emma was sorry, for Zandra's face turned even whiter and she flinched visibly.

"I'm sorry, Zan," she went on quickly, "but I cannot understand why you are making so much out of an absence that, at most, will last no longer than a few days. Jason told you repeatedly that there was no danger involved, and that he would return almost immediately. One day already has passed, and he probably will return within the next two to three days. If you don't get over your case of the dismals, you'll greet him looking like one of Macbeth's witches."

For the first time, Zandra laughed. "I suppose you are right. Jason called me superstitious and tried to make a joke of it, but Emma, I had the worst premonition when he left. As I watched him walk to the street and get into the carriage, I was sure that I was seeing him for the last time, that something terrible would happen and he would not return from France."

"You should have listened to Jason and not your premonition," Emma told her. "Believe me, if there had been any risk involved, Jason would not have gone, certainly not at this time. He is every bit as desirous of being with you as you are of being with him. I never saw a man who so doted on a woman as Jason does on you."

This, also, brought a smile of pleasure to Zandra's wan face. But she knew that no matter how much her husband missed her, it could not possibly be more than she had missed him last night. She had lain in the big bed for hours, thinking only how vast and empty it seemed without him, how empty her arms were without him, how empty her life was without him. Unable to sleep and too nervous to lie quietly in bed, she had spent what seemed an endless amount of time pacing about in the bedchamber. Once she had opened one of the clothespresses just to look at his clothing, and took out one of his coats and held it against her cheek. "Come back, oh, come back soon," she had breathed into the woolly garment. She returned to the bed only when she felt ready to drop from sheer exhaustion. Even then, she had slept only fitfully.

"You are right, Emma," she said finally. "I am making much too much out of this. I *am* being silly." And then she picked up her cup and sipped determinedly at her tea.

As she and Emma were leaving the parlor, Samuel, the butler, appeared in the doorway bearing on a tray a small white card with a crest on one side and something written on the other. Emma picked it up.

"Why, it is Lady Dysart's card," she said in surprise. "She invites us to tea with her and Lady Lawring this afternoon."

"Oh, bother!" Zandra made a face. "I'm sure Lord Dysart told her she must entertain us, otherwise she would not so much as look in our direction. If the messenger is still waiting, Samuel, tell him to give Lady Dysart our regrets."

"Tell him to tell Lady Dysart that we appreciate the invitation and will be most pleased to join her and Lady Lawring for tea." Emma gave the counterorder like an officer plunging into the thick of battle.

"But Emma—" Zandra began.

"Hush!" Emma said sternly. "I am not going to sit here and watch you pace around the house like a caged animal. I think half your trouble is boredom, and whatever else you may be at the Dysart residence, you will not be bored."

"Hardly," Zandra said, "with two old dowagers looking down their noses at me, while I try valiantly to keep from insulting them. Gower's mother likes me even less than Lady Dysart."

"You are safely out of her son's reach now,"

Emma pointed out, "so she has no reason to dislike you. Besides, I don't think she ever did dislike you; she was merely afraid you were going to marry her son. Mothers seldom like the women who, in their opinion, replace them in their sons' hearts."

"I will let you know how it is when I have a son of my own," Zandra said, her spirits suddenly lifting. By the time they returned from tea, the second day of Jason's absence would be over and that would be the halfway point. If she kept thinking about it that way, she would be able to get through the rest of the time without too much difficulty.

"All right, Samuel," Zandra said, looking up and discovering him still waiting there. "Tell Lady Dysart we will be delighted." When he had gone, she said to Emma, "I am afraid that living next door to the Dysarts is going to make me into a terrible liar."

Gower finished the letter he had been struggling to write for the past hour and nodded approvingly. He had worded it just right. He got up from his writing desk and stretched. He would deliver the letter himself first thing in the morning.

There was no chance that the duke could return by tomorrow and only the faintest possibility that he could return the following day, but Gower was not willing to risk even the slightest chance of faulty timing; therefore it was better to be a bit early setting his plan in motion than to wait too long.

He folded the letter and put it in one of his crested envelopes. It was late and he needed a good night's sleep because tomorrow was going to be one of the most important days of his life.

As he undressed and put on his nightshirt, his heart began to pound as though it were trying to leap out of his chest. He sat on the side of the bed almost gasping for breath. For the span of three minutes he considered abandoning his scheme. What if something went wrong? What if he were found out? He could be held up for ridicule not only in London but throughout the whole country. Or even worse, he could be prosecuted and sent to Newgate, depending upon how far his plan had progressed before he was discovered. He would not survive a week at Newgate and his family would not survive the scandal.

He took a deep breath and then another. But the plan must succeed; it had been too well thought out. The possibility of failure didn't even exist.

Holding desperately to that thought, he lay down, carefully arranging the quilts and pillows, and finally went to sleep. He did not awaken until his valet shook him the next morning.

At ten o'clock he was lifting the big knocker on the front door of the duke's house. When

Samuel opened the door, Gower bid him a cheerful good morning and asked to see Mrs. Wallace. "Tell her Lord Lawring is calling on a matter of some urgency."

Samuel hesitated a moment as though trying to decide whether to usher the uninvited visitor inside. Finally, the title no doubt influencing him, he said, "Will you step inside, my lord? I will see if Mrs. Wallace is available."

Emma appeared in the reception hall almost immediately, her face plainly revealing her surprise.

"Good morning, Gower. Samuel said you wanted to see me about some urgent matter. Won't you come into the morning room and have tea with Zandra and me?"

"No, thank you, I haven't time," he said pleasantly, remembering to behave as cheerfully as possible in case there should be questions later about his frame of mind. He took the letter he had written last night from his coat. "Would you please give this letter to the duke when he returns? I would appreciate it more than you know."

Emma took the letter, turned it over in her hands and looked at the crest, then the address. "Why not wait until he returns and say whatever you have to say to him in person?" she asked practically. "We expect his return in a matter of days." It seemed odd and unnecessary for Gower to give her a letter to give to Jason.

"Oh, I thought you knew the situation, Mrs. Wallace," Gower said quickly. "There has been bad blood between us and this letter is my way of trying to straighten out the matter."

"Very well. I shall be glad to see that Jason gets your letter," Emma agreed. "I don't like to see enmity linger between people."

"Nor do I," Gower said. "Now I wonder if I might speak to Zandra for a moment. There are some things that need to be straightened out between us also."

Emma gave him a long look. He was smiling benignly and was evidently in a conciliatory mood. "That will be up to Zandra," she said.

"Of course."

"Then you will join us in the morning room?"

"No, please . . . if Zandra would come out here . . . private matter, you see." He must not get flustered, he told himself. He must not let his growing nervousness show now that he had reached the crucial part of his plan.

"I will see," Emma said and left the hall.

It was fully five minutes before Zandra appeared. Gower sucked in his breath; she looked more beautiful than he had ever seen her. True, she was a trifle pale, but that made her green eyes darker and gave her a fragile look, like some priceless, delicate treasure.

He wanted nothing more in the world than to clasp her to him and make love to her until they both were too exhausted even for words. But that would have to wait for just a little while, just until . . .

"Zandra." He rushed across the wide hall to her and took both her hands in his. She pulled away instantly, and what he saw in her face then did not please him. Dislike? Disgust? He was sure only that seeing him gave her no pleasure and that he would have to be more careful.

He took her hands again, holding them firmly this time. "My uncle, Lord Dysart, has sent me to tell you . . ." he paused for just the fraction of a second, ". . . tell you that there has been an accident."

Her already pale face immediately lost any sign of color. "What? Where?" she whispered. She did not have to ask to whom the accident had happened. She had known all along, but yesterday she had foolishly put her "premonition" in the back of her mind, reassuring herself with mere words.

"Oh, my dear, I hate having to tell you this." Gower squeezed her hands. "The duke's boat went down near the coast of England."

"Oh, my God!" she cried. "Jason's dead!"

"No, no," he said quickly. "He was rescued." Seeing that she seemed about to faint, he let go of her hands and took her by the shoulders, shaking her slightly. "He is alive, Zandra. The duke is alive, but he is grievously hurt and is calling for you."

"Where—where is he?" She barely managed to get the words out.

"My uncle has asked me to take you to him. At once! There is no time to lose."

"Yes, yes, at once!" The words galvanized her to action. She ran to the bench beside the stairway and snatched up the cloak she had dropped there when she and Emma had come in yesterday afternoon. Gower helped her put it on, then took her arm and steered her quickly out of the house.

Tears were running down her face, though she was unaware that she was crying. Why had she let him go? Somehow she could have made him stay with her if she had insisted. She had known something terrible was going to happen and she had let him go anyway.

Oh, God, don't let it be too late; let me get to him before it's too late, she prayed. Don't let him die; don't take Jason away from me . . .

Gower helped her into his carriage and motioned for the driver to start. He settled beside Zandra and put his arm around her to comfort her. "There, there, sweet one, don't worry. Everything is going to be all right. I give you my word that everything will be just fine now."

She looked out at the street. "Oh, Gower, can't we go faster? We must *hurry*."

Gower signaled the driver to apply the whip freely. He had never imagined that Zandra— cool, clearheaded, calm Zandra—could ever be so panicked and distraught. He gave a long sigh of satisfaction. Her panic had worked in his favor: she had left the house in such a frenzy of terror that she had not said a word to anyone, not even her aunt.

Chapter Fourteen

JASON, SHIVERING WITH THE COLD, PULLED the carriage robe more tightly about him. The return crossing had not been as rough but it had been much colder, and even now, miles away from the coast, he could still feel the damp chill through to his very bones.

In spite of his discomfort he felt elated. It was all just as he had imagined it several days ago in Calais: leaving the boat, getting into the carriage that Lord Dysart had had waiting at the tiny port every day since Jason left, telling the coachman to hurry, hurry back to London. Now he was on Ratcliffe Highway, only a matter of minutes from the Tower of London; thence they would continue down several different streets through the heart of town, then onto Mount Street and

. . . home! He wondered if Zandra would hear the carriage and come running out to meet him. It could be that she had expected him as early as yesterday and was sitting on the window seat in their bedchamber looking up and down the street for the first sight of the carriage. Now he could hold her in his arms and they could laugh together about her forebodings that had amounted to naught.

It was only mid-afternoon, but already the dark, low-hanging clouds made it feel like early evening. They were snow clouds, and by late night the city probably would be blanketed. How good it would be to sit before a roaring fire with Zandra on his lap! Never again would he go anywhere without her.

The carriage turned from the Strand into Haymarket and then Piccadilly. Only a couple minutes now. His heart was racing far ahead of the horses by the time they turned onto Mount Street. He leaped from the carriage before it came to a complete stop at his house and was at the front door in four long strides. He was halfway across the reception hall before Samuel appeared, breathed a sigh of relief, and said, "Oh, sir, welcome home."

Jason barely got out a "thank you" before asking, "Where is the duchess?"

He heard a door open upstairs, and then Emma came running down the stairs to meet him. "Jason, thank God you're here!"

If it had been cold on the channel and in the carriage, it suddenly felt like the farthest reaches of the Antarctic in the hall. He froze where he stood. "What is wrong?" he asked, scarcely above a whisper. "Where is Zandra? What has happened?" There was no doubt, from the look on Emma's face, that something was badly amiss.

"She's . . . not here," Emma said hesitantly. "I don't know where she is."

"What do you mean you don't know where she is?" Jason asked uncomprehendingly. "Where *is* she?"

"Come into the salon," Emma said. "We must talk."

What in God's name was going on? Jason wondered. He had recovered somewhat from his original fright and was beginning to be a trifle annoyed with Emma for acting so mysterious. He knew full well that if anything serious had happened to Zandra, Emma would not be as composed as she was.

Emma carefully closed the door of the salon behind them. "To be perfectly truthful, Jason, I am not sure whether I should be frantic with worry or simply furious with Zandra and Gower."

"Gower!" Jason roared. "What has that . . . that brash zealot to do with Zandra?"

"I am not sure. Sit down and I will tell you

210

what I know." Emma told him how Gower had come to the house two days ago and given her a letter to give him, then asked to speak to Zandra alone. "Zandra left the house with him and she has not returned. The truth is . . ." Her lower lip began to tremble. "I cannot find her, and I've looked everywhere I can think of."

Was the woman mad? She sounded as though she had misplaced some object. "You are not making sense, Emerald. Zandra would never go off with Gower."

"But she did. Samuel saw her get into Gower's carriage with him and drive away." Emma's eyes were wet now. She felt like a child being lectured for being irresponsible. "I found out from Lady Dysart where Gower's rooms are and I sent Samuel there. No one was there but Gower's valet and he said Gower had gone away and would not be back until sometime next week."

"The letter," Jason remembered. "You said Gower left a letter for me."

"Oh—yes." Emma went to the mantel, picked up the letter and gave it to Jason.

He opened it in great haste. After reading it through, he whispered, "Good God! It isn't possible." Then he read the letter again and handed it to Emma.

She read it through without blinking, then read it again.

Your Grace:

I must tell you at once that Zandra has come to the conclusion that marrying you a second time was a tremendous mistake on her part. She sincerely regrets any hurt or inconvenience it may cause you, but she is most anxious for a divorce. She has stated that it is immaterial to her whether you divorce her or she you; however, it might be easier for everyone if you arrange the bill of divorcement this time.

By the time you read this, Zandra will have left with me and will once again be my mistress. Again, we regret whatever distress this may cause you, but we can no longer thwart our desire to be together.

Gower, Lord Lawring

"This is insane," she said after the second reading. "She would never run away with Gower."

Jason stared at the wall, aware only of a stabbing pain that seemed to tear through his whole body. "Not even to be his mistress . . . again?" he asked.

"That's what is insane!" Emma cried. "She was *never* his mistress. He wanted her to be and she refused him. Think, Jason! Can you imagine Zandra and Gower—" She broke off.

"Of course not." He banged his fist down on

a table. "It is as I thought in the beginning: that wretch has kidnapped her!"

"Kidnapped?" Emma looked as though she did not quite know what the word meant.

"This letter is nothing but one vile lie after another," Jason said. "Samuel!"

When the butler did not appear immediately, Jason roared, "Samuel, come here!"

Samuel appeared in the doorway, his face as unexpressive as he could make it.

"Yes, Your Grace?" he said.

"Mrs. Wallace tells me you saw Lord Lawring kidnap my wife," Jason said.

Samuel's eyebrows drew up an inch. Otherwise, he showed no sign of surprise as he said, "Kidnap, sir?"

"Tell me about it," Jason demanded. "Tell me what was said, what happened from the minute that bas—Lord Lawring put his foot in this house."

"Well, sir, he knocked at the door and asked to see Mrs. Wallace." Samuel gazed at the ceiling, trying to remember exactly. "Said to tell her it was a matter of some urgency. I delivered the message and she went out to the hall to speak with him. I went to the back of the house then, so I . . ."

Jason held up his hand. "Exactly what did he say to you, Emma, when he gave you the letter?"

"I asked him why he didn't say whatever he had to say to you in person, and he said there had been bad blood between you and this was his way of making amends . . . or something like that. I took the letter and then he asked to speak to Zandra, saying he wanted to make things right with her, also. We had been sitting in the morning room, so I went back and asked Zandra if she wanted to talk to him and she said no. No hesitation at all. She didn't even think twice, she just said no. I told her it might be better if she did. You see, Gower seemed so . . . I don't know . . . cheerful, almost elated, and I thought that if he was willing to make peace Zandra should meet him halfway. I finally persuaded her to go talk to him. When she didn't return after a long time, I went into the hall and neither of them was there. Samuel was standing at the window and I asked him if Zandra had gone upstairs after Gower left, and he told me she had left with him."

Jason looked at Samuel again. "You actually saw them leave together?"

"Yes, sir." Samuel nodded. "I thought I heard the front door close, so I came back to the hall to see if the visitor had left. I went to the window and I saw Lord Lawring and the duchess rushing to the carriage . . ."

"Rushing?" Jason said sharply. "Was Lord Lawring forcing her to go? Did she seem reluctant?"

Samuel was silent for a moment. He considered telling a small lie, but he could not see that it would help matters, so looking down at the floor he said, "She was not at all reluctant, sir. She went with him willingly. For a fact, she seemed in a mighty hurry, as though she did not want to be stopped by anything or anybody."

"Thank you. That will be all, Samuel," Jason said curtly.

Samuel bowed and left the room, his heart leaden.

"I don't understand it," Emma said. "I don't understand it at all." She looked at Jason and inhaled sharply. "No, Jason, it is *not* what you are thinking. She would *never* run away with Gower. Dear Lord, don't you know how much she loved you?"

"Loved?" Jason repeated the word. "I see you use the past tense."

"Oh, Jason, be reasonable," Emma pleaded.

"That is exactly what I am trying to be," he said. "I cannot believe Zandra would willingly go anywhere with Gower. But I know Samuel does not lie, and he saw it all."

At that moment Samuel appeared in the door again. "Your Grace, Lord Dysart is here to see you."

Jason looked up, uncomprehending at first. "Lord Dysart?" he repeated as though he had never heard the name before. The affair of the Pretender was at that moment so far from his mind that even the names connected with it did not strike a familiar chord. Then his mind

215

clicked into action: Lord Dysart, Gower's uncle! "Show him in at once, Samuel."

"Jason!" His lordship entered at a fast clip, hand outstretched to the younger man. "I happened to be looking out a window and saw your baggage being brought in. I gather you have just arrived." Then, noticing Emma for the first time, he bowed. "Good afternoon, Mrs. Wallace. I trust you and the duchess are well."

"Sit down, please, Lord Dysart," Jason said calmly. "Yes, I have just come in and have found a passing strange situation here." He thought it better to understate the case until he found out more of the facts.

"What is that, Jason?" Lord Dysart asked. It was obvious he was merely being polite, impatient to know the outcome of Jason's mission.

"My wife apparently has been kidnapped by your nephew."

It took a few seconds for the sentence, spoken in a flat tone of voice, to register. "What? What is that you say?"

"Zandra has been kidnapped by Gower."

"Impossible!" Lord Dysart sputtered.

"I am afraid not, sir." Jason was striving to keep his temper and his voice under control. "Both Emma and my butler talked with Gower when he came here to the house two days ago, and Samuel saw him leave with my wife."

"I cannot believe Gower would kidnap anyone," Lord Dysart said, disbelief in his eyes. "Frankly, I do not think the boy has that much gumption. And why, pray tell, would he *want* to kidnap Zandra? Yes, I know," he added quickly, "that she is a beautiful—more than beautiful—woman, and that Gower was much interested in her not long ago. But surely you cannot believe the boy would abscond with another man's wife!"

"He was seen—" Jason began, then stopped. Dysart's last statement made it clear what he thought: if the two had gone away together, it had to be voluntary on Zandra's part.

"You say she has been gone for two days?" Lord Dysart asked.

"A little more than two days, for she left in the morning," Emma said.

"There is some mistake, a misunderstanding." His lordship stated it firmly, as though suddenly possessed of extra knowledge about the disappearance. "I will send for Gower and he can explain . . ."

"Your nephew is not in town," Emma said tersely. "His man said he would be away until next week."

"I had not heard of any journey he was planning," Lord Dysart said, "but I am not often made privy to his comings and goings. My wife would know more."

Jason had remained quiet during this exchange. It was obvious that Dysart, and even Samuel, thought Zandra had gone with

Gower of her own free will. Only Emma kept protesting, saying how much Zandra loved Jason and would never willingly leave him . . . and it would not surprise him if even Emma were beginning to have doubts.

After all, Zandra had a muddied reputation. Could that reputation be deserved? Jason winced at the thought. Was her great love for him only pretense? She had run away from him once; was she not capable of doing it again? In his letter, Gower had said Zandra wanted to become his mistress once again. Had she been his mistress until he, Jason, appeared on the scene and offered better prospects? Emma had said no—as naturally she would.

One thing was certain. If Zandra had indeed left of her own free will, then she must return the same way. But what if she did not return? And what if she did—would he want to take her back a second time? He would have to think long and hard on that when he was alone.

But what if Zandra *had* been kidnapped by Gower? Unlikely, illogical as it seemed, it was the thought he wanted to cling to.

"Jason, I realize this is not the best of times to discuss what happened in France," Lord Dysart was saying, "but I must know."

Jason responded as if in a daze. "Yes, yes. I understand. The news I bring is not good, sir." He paused to allow the older man to prepare himself for what was likely to be one of the greatest disappointments of his life. "James absolutely refused to sign the declaration. He offered to write a declaration of his own, giving English Protestants what he called 'reasonable security,' but he would not —and made it clear that he never will— renounce the Catholic Church."

"I was afraid of that, yet I had hoped . . ." Lord Dysart broke off. He remained quiet for a long time, his facial expression reflecting the thoughts that went through his mind. Finally he said, "So be it. I think you and I should take the news of his refusal to sign the declaration to the Queen at Windsor. Can you be ready to leave in the morning?"

"But I . . ." Jason began. He had not thought out his plans completely, but he was of half a mind to set out on a search for Zandra even though he had no idea where to look. "All right, sir," he said distractedly. "I will be ready to leave at whatever hour you say."

Chapter Fifteen

THE JOURNEY FROM LONDON TO WINDSOR WAS a strained one. Viscount Bolingbroke accompanied Jason and Lord Dysart and insisted on hearing a full account of Jason's trip.

"Jason believes James would be a weak and ineffectual ruler," Lord Dysart said flatly, answering for Jason. "I am willing to accept his appraisal of the situation; otherwise I would not have asked him to go in the first place."

Bolingbroke nodded solemnly. Though he did not know Jason well, he had the utmost respect for Dysart's judgment and knew he must trust his opinion.

While the two men conversed, Jason stared out disconsolately at the landscape. He had scarcely closed his eyes last night as thoughts raced through his mind, over and over. Zandra had been kidnapped, she had *not* been kidnapped, she had been Gower's mistress, she had *not* been Gower's mistress.

He had no more idea now than he had had yesterday what to believe. There would not have been a moment's doubt in his mind about what had happened had it not been for Samuel's testimony. The butler's words raged through his mind like a fire out of control: *She was not at all reluctant, sir. She went with him willingly. For a fact, she seemed in a mighty hurry, as though she did not want to be stopped by anything or anybody.*

But for those words, he would have torn apart England, Scotland, Ireland and Wales looking for her.

He clenched his fists at his sides. Unless he stopped thinking about it, he would go insane. He tried to concentrate on what his two companions were saying.

". . . only a matter of time," Dysart was concluding.

Knowing he referred to the Queen's life, Jason asked, "How much time?" For months, years even, it had been reported that it was "only a matter of time" before Anne died.

"According to the last report, a week or two, if that long," Bolingbroke said. "If only the succession could have been settled on a happier note before her demise!"

"We're almost there," Dysart said.

The turrets of Windsor Castle were now visible from the road. The castle stood on a cliff above the Thames, towering over the village. The massive connecting buildings loomed like an impenetrable fortress.

The carriage entered the courtyard nearest the private apartments, the quarters of the royal family. A footman was instantly on hand to help the three gentlemen alight and usher them inside. They were offered refreshments and a small but comfortable room in which to wait until the Queen felt disposed to see them.

Dysart distracted Jason by pointing out various historical aspects of the palace, but he stopped abruptly when a footman approached. Bolingbroke stepped forward and spoke with the man for a moment, then returned to the group. "The Queen is unable to leave her bed, but she will see us in the royal bedchamber for a very few minutes."

They followed the footman down a long corridor, up a stairway and down another corridor. He knocked gently at a door, which was immediately opened by a woman beautifully dressed in a deep red velvet gown and a small white cap of the most delicate lace.

"Is Her Majesty ready, Mrs. Hill?" the footman asked.

The woman nodded. "She will see them now." She turned to the three visitors. "I must warn you, you can stay only a short time. The Queen is very weak today."

As they went from the Queen's private sitting room into the royal bedchamber, Dysart whispered to Jason, "That is Abigail Hill, the Queen's favorite lady-in-waiting."

His first glimpse of the Queen, propped up by many pillows in the large canopied bed, caused Jason to stop in his tracks. He had thought she looked ill at the supper at the Banqueting House only recently, but now she looked to be knocking at death's door. And there was no question that the door would be opened very soon.

"Come in, gentlemen," she said weakly, "and tell me what news you bring of James."

It was Bolingbroke who spoke. "I will be brief, Your Majesty. Your half brother has again refused to sign the declaration. He will not give up his faith."

The Queen nodded. "As I thought."

"The Duke of Melford says he would not give an inch—except to say that if he was brought back to England, he would give the Protestants what he called reasonable security."

"Not enough," the Queen whispered. "Without his signature on the document, no promise would be kept." She turned her face toward the far wall, obviously not wanting the visitors to look upon whatever emotion she was feeling.

The three men were uncertain what to do. Then Mrs. Hill entered the room and motioned for them to leave. "You may stay the night if you like," she said. "It is beginning to snow and the road may be impassable before you can get back to London."

"No," Jason said quickly. "Thank you for your hospitable offer, but I must return home."

Dysart looked out the window. "But Jason, there is a good chance you cannot get to London. Look how it is snowing already. I think we should remain."

"I can't take the chance that we might be snowed in," Jason told his neighbor. "I am sure you understand that I must be at home." Dysart nodded.

Jason, thinking that too much time already had been wasted with nothing accomplished, left the castle hastily to begin the long and possibly perilous journey back to London. As he got into the carriage, he prayed silently: Let her be at home when I get there. Please God, let her be waiting for me.

Chapter Sixteen

BEFORE JASON WAS MORE THAN A FEW MILES from Windsor the snow was swirling down in dense clouds. He had only to look at the coachman to know whether the flakes were sticking. Within a half hour, the man resembled a snowman; only his face visible beneath the brim of his hat proved he was human. Both men knew that long before London was sighted, they would not be able to see the road. The journey would last hours longer than under normal circumstances. Yet Jason felt he *must* return to London tonight. Something inside him urged him on and on.

Was that the way Zandra had felt with her premonition? He had been wrong to try to tease her out of her fears, to leave her when she had felt so strongly about his going. And she had been right, had she not? Something dreadful *had* happened.

Was it possible that everything that had occurred had been planned well in advance? Had Zandra and Gower been scheming together behind his back? He hated himself for his thoughts, but the whole terrible business seemed to be falling into place. Looking back, he could see how she had arranged everything. By talking constantly about the "something" that she was afraid was going to happen she had been, in a very subtle way, preparing his mind for it. Only he had thought she was concerned for *his* safety, little dreaming that it was when he returned he would find catastrophe.

His thoughts stopped abruptly. Was what he was thinking possible? Would Zandra, his loving, adorable Zandra, really have plotted against him like that? He slumped in the seat of the gently rocking carriage, remembering Gower's letter. *Zandra has come to the conclusion that marrying you a second time was a tremendous mistake . . . By the time you read this, Zandra will have left with me and will once again be my mistress.*

But it was Samuel's words that convinced him more than anything else that Zandra had left him for Gower. And all the love she had given him, was that just playacting? He could not believe that anyone could feign desire and passion to that extent. Perhaps when she first had come back into his life she honestly had wanted him and had wanted to be married to him a second time, but afterward . . . Was there something about her that made it impossible for her to be true to one man? Or was it something in himself, something about him that made it impossible for Zandra to be true to him?

He remembered all too vividly how it had been after Zandra left him that first time after only one night. There had been the gibes of his peers, the sly winks: "Were you too much for her or was she too much for *you*, Jase?" and, "After only one night? What did you show the girl that scared her so?" Even worse were the eyes of his servants, some amused, some curious, others contemptuous, and still others, like his valet Jeremiah's, as sorrowful as though there had been a death. That was how Samuel had looked at him as he related Zandra's departure.

By God, he was not going to go through all that again! He simply was not!

He looked out at the landscape, then tapped on the little window, indicating to the driver that they should halt.

"Yes, sir?"

"Come down and sit in the carriage," Jason instructed. "I will drive now."

"But, sir—"

"Do as I say!" Jason pulled his coat tightly about him and got up on the high seat. When he saw that the other man was situated inside, he started the team. The poor man needed a chance to thaw out, while he needed activity, anything to keep his mind off Zandra.

It was not long before it was impossible to see the road, but Jason followed the path where the forest had been cut back. He stared straight ahead, trying to concentrate on the ever-deepening snow and the wretched condition of the road. In spite of his increasing discomfort in body and mind, he refused to stop at any of the several inns along the way. He was determined to get back to London even if he had to abandon the team and carriage and walk. Thoughts about Zandra still seeped into his mind like water through cracks in a dam. No matter how he fought against it, he could not stop the flow of images: how she looked with her dark auburn hair spread across a white pillow, her beautifully shaped body arching to his touch, the feel of her arms encircling him as they merged into one. "Oh, God, I am not going to hurt like that again," he muttered softly.

No more, he thought. Never again.

By the time they reached the outskirts of London, dusk had turned to dark. The horses, already weary two hours past, now looked ready to drop in their tracks. Along the streets of the city the snow remained unsullied, with few carriage tracks visible.

The carriage Jason drove was Bolingbroke's and the driver his man, so as they entered Mount Street, Jason told the coachman to go straight to the Bolingbroke house and lose no time in rubbing down the team and putting them up for the night.

There was fear in the man's eyes as he said to Jason, "You won't be telling the viscount that *you* drove *me* in the carriage, now will you?"

"It isn't likely the subject will ever come up," Jason said. He hurried into the house, feeling wet and frozen to the bone.

"What news?" he asked instantly as Emma met him in the wide hall.

"None at all," she said. "I was hoping you would have some, that maybe Lord Dysart knows . . ."

"He knows nothing," Jason said, disappointed in spite of the miles and miles he had spent trying to prepare himself for just such disappointment. "We know more than he, which is little or nothing."

"Jason, you are drenched and shivering," Emma said worriedly. "Go at once to your room and I will have Jeremiah prepare a hot bath for you and then Cook will make some hot broth. Why in the name of every-thing holy did the three of you try to come back in this weather?"

"The three of us didn't," he told her.

"Your mind has slipped its moorings," she said seriously, "but never mind, I understand. Now go." She pointed up the stairway as though directing a small child.

Jason reappeared in the small salon an hour later and stood before the roaring fire that Emma had had Samuel set as soon as Jason had gone upstairs. He had had a steaming bath, put on dry clothes, drunk Cook's hot broth and eaten a hearty supper. Now, with a brandy snifter in his hand, he felt warm for the first time since leaving Windsor.

"Well, Emerald," he said after a few min-utes of silence, "I suppose there will be just the two of us here from now on. I don't know if, under the circumstances, you wish to stay, but I want you to know you are welcome. I imagine that once Zandra is settled wherever she and Lord Lawring—"

"Dear Lord!" Emma cried, throwing her hands in the air, "The man's brains have congealed in the cold weather! He has not an ounce of sense but has turned to ice."

Jason gave her a thin smile. "I am merely trying to be practical. I have grown fond of you and I do not want you to think I would put you out of my house because your niece has chosen to leave you behind this time."

"Jason, will you stop rattling on in this manner?" Emma pushed him down in a chair and then stood over him. "No matter what you think, no matter how it looks, Zandra did not go off with Gower willingly. If she left here without force on his part, it was because of some trick. I *know* my niece and I know how much she loves you."

"Emma, she does not—"

"Hush now, and let me finish," she interrupted. "She loves you more than life. Even during those years when she thought she would never see you again, she could not get you out of her mind. Because of that, no other man interested her. Not even Gower. I watched her from the day she met him, trying to make herself fall in love with him. She never even came close to succeeding. Gower's letter just shows him for the liar he is. I've already told you he tried to get her to become his mistress and she sent him away and told him she didn't ever want to see him again. I also told you how reluctant she was to see him that day he came here. I had to push her to the door. Oh, if only I hadn't! If only I had respected her wish never to see him again!"

"What trick could he possibly have used to make her go off with him?" Jason asked. He wanted more than anything to believe Emma, but he still could not imagine Zandra falling for any ruse he might devise.

"I haven't a notion," she said. "My mind is

not as devious as his, so how could I know his schemes?"

Jason thought about this for a moment. "You say you sent Samuel to his lodgings to find him?"

"Yes. His valet reported that he was out of town and would be back next week, as I told you," she said.

"If he's a liar, his valet could be also." Jason stood up. "Tell Samuel to have my carriage brought around." He started up the stairs for his coat and boots.

"Jason, you are not going out tonight!" Emma cried. "It is late, very late, and you already have been chilled to the bone once today. Besides, the snow hasn't let up at all."

"Tell me where Gower lives," was his only answer.

Emma tried pleading, but to no avail. Jason was determined to go at once. Emma had almost convinced him of Zandra's fidelity and love. He *had* to find out whatever he could at Gower's. His exhaustion was of no consequence, and in his own carriage with a fresh horse, he felt the trip across town to Exeter Street, where Samuel had said Gower lived, would not take too long despite the deep snow.

The going was not too bad for the first few blocks, but then the snow suddenly seemed to deepen at Piccadilly. He got out of the carriage, pulled the reins over the horse's head, and led the animal for the next two blocks.

When he reached the Strand, he tied the horse to a corner hitching post and walked the block and a half to Gower's rooms on the top floor of a rather dilapidated house.

He went up the steep steps at the side of the house as Samuel had told him to, then peered through the large glass pane on the door. It was as black as the depths of hell inside. There was no sound from within. Though the hour was late, it was not yet bedtime for most of London, certainly not for a rounder like Gower. Jason rapped on the door, waited, then rapped again much louder. There was still no movement within. He tried the door and was not surprised to find it locked. He walked slowly back down the stairs. Obviously Gower had not returned from wherever he had gone.

He trudged back to the corner where he had left the horse and carriage. Suddenly the exhaustion of the long day all but overcame him. He hardly had the strength to climb up to the high seat of the carriage.

He flicked the reins over the horse's back and started home, but had got little more than a block down the Strand when the horse slipped on a sheet of ice and fell.

"Damn!" Jason swore under his breath. The horse was struggling to get back to its feet, but the slickness of the street made that impossible. Jason climbed down, but there seemed to be no way to assist the horse. He took off his long coat and tried putting it beneath the horse's front feet to give it a foothold that did not skid, but the coat slipped across the ice under the horse's hooves.

"Yer wasting yer toime, mister," said a voice close by.

It belonged to a man who was standing in the shadow of a building nearby. "Could you help me here?" Jason said. "I will make it worth your time." Knowing nothing of the stranger's integrity, or lack of it, Jason had no intention of showing him money now. "*Very* worth your time," he said.

The man was thoughtful for a minute, then said, "All right, gov'ner, but I'll take 'alf now."

"I have nothing with me now," he said. "You will get it all when you get to Mount Street with my horse and carriage."

"And 'ow be yer getting there?"

"The same way the horse would if it could get up—hoofing it." Certainly it would be impossible to get a hackney carriage now. The man reluctantly agreed to the arrangement.

Jason started out through the snow, already so weary he could scarcely put one foot in front of the other. But he trudged on, down one street and then another, on the circuitous route home. Somewhere along the way he became vaguely aware that his mind seemed to be fading in and out, like a distant voice that, from time to time, became garbled or almost inaudible. One minute he was thinking about Gower and Zandra, the next minute he was seeing Queen Anne propped up in the huge bed by many pillows. All at once he became terribly warm and he removed the wet coat, then wiped perspiration from his forehead. But before he had gone a full block, he was freezing cold again and so he put the coat back on.

At one point he was unsure he was even going in the right direction. The snow was falling harder and it was almost impossible to distinguish familiar landmarks. Finally he recognized Jermyn Street. He was a block from Piccadilly. He walked on, his steps becoming slower.

Had she been tricked? *Could* she be tricked, bright, intelligent Zandra? Would she renounce her faith in Gower and be Queen? No, that was something else, somebody else . . .

Instinct and the last of his faltering strength got him to Mount Street. He was aware of making one last effort to open the front door, then he remembered no more. As he collapsed, he was kept from falling by Samuel's outstretched arms.

"Mrs. Wallace, he is here," Samuel called, and Emma came running into the hall, saying, "Jason, where in heaven's name have you been? A man brought your horse and carriage home an hour ago and—Oh, my God!" She arrived just as Samuel was laying Jason gently upon the bench beside the stairway.

Stooping and placing her hand on his forehead, she said, "He is burning with fever. Help me, Samuel, we must get him to bed at once."

Samuel called a footman and between them, they carried Jason to his bedchamber, undressed him, and put him to bed. As soon as he was in bed, Jason began muttering.

Emma bent down and put her ear near his mouth, but the words she heard made no sense. She felt his forehead again and this time he was as cold as death. She turned to the footman and said, "Go at once for his doctor."

"Excuse me, ma'am," Samuel said, "but the duke doesn't have a doctor here. He has been in London only a short while and—"

"Then go for *any* doctor, the nearest one," Emma ordered.

"I doubt you'll get one to come at this hour in all the snow," Samuel said.

Emma went to the window and looked out. "I suppose we'll have to wait until morning. Bring me every blanket and comforter you can find, Samuel, before he shakes the bed down with his chill."

Finally, seeing that there was nothing else to do for him at present, she sent the two men to bed while she sat beside Jason for the rest of the night, now only a matter of three hours.

He spoke from time to time, sometimes calling loudly for Zandra over and over, until Emma found tears coursing down her cheeks. At first light, Samuel went for a doctor, leaving Emma still sitting beside the delirious man.

Chapter Seventeen

IT WAS PNEUMONIA, DR. BOYLSTON TOLD Emma, and Jason's condition was critical. He was quiet now, except for his breathing—long, rasping breaths that seemed to come from the very depths of him. He did not speak except for a scarcely audible whisper from time to time. When Emma put her ear to his lips to hear what he was saying, she heard but one word: "Zandra."

Even as Jason slipped in and out of consciousness, calling for her, Zandra also lay in bed, hot tears scalding the corners of her eyes as she longed for Jason. It had finally occurred to her that she was being held by a madman and that with every day that passed, her chances of ever seeing her husband again grew slimmer. She had given up almost all hope of escape. She also had given up excoriating herself for falling for his ploy; she had been in such a state of shock on hearing that Jason's boat had sunk that all common sense had deserted her. She still was not sure, in fact, whether his boat *had* sunk and Gower had used that opportunity to get her away, or whether Gower had made it all up, a miserable lie. When she asked him which was the truth, he only smiled at her, the truth buried deep behind his veiled eyes.

She had realized soon after leaving the house that morning that Gower was not taking her to Jason at all. The carriage had turned from Oxford Street into Tottenham Court Road, which went due north, rather than into one of the streets that went east or south to the coast. She was slumped against the cushion, her hands clenched so tightly in her lap that her fingernails cut into her palms. Suddenly she sat up, looking out at the street, then at Gower who sat opposite her. "Where are we going?" she asked. "This is not the way to the coast."

"We are not going to the coast," Gower said quietly. "Jason is not there."

"Where is he?" The panic she felt caused her voice to crack. Was it possible that Gower was not taking her to Jason?

"I am not sure."

"What do you mean, you are not sure?" She was nearly screaming at him now.

"Sit back and relax, Zandra. It will take us some time to reach our destination."

She was sure now that wherever Gower was taking her was somewhere she did not want to be and nowhere near Jason. She fumbled with the handle of the door.

Gower caught her hand in his. "Just what do you think you're doing?"

"You are going to tell the coachman to stop this instant and I am getting out."

"Don't be foolish! We are not stopping and you are not getting out until we get to the inn."

"What inn?"

Gower only smiled.

She jerked her hands out of his, reached for the door handle again and at the same time threw her weight against the door. She would have fallen out had not Gower caught her around the waist just as the door swung open.

"Get your hands off me!" she cried. "I am not going anywhere with you. If Jason is hurt—"

"Stop worrying about Jason and sit still," he said sternly, as though giving orders to a child.

That was when she first began to wonder whether he was lying or taking advantage of a tragic situation. "Jason's boat did not sink, did it?" she accused him. "You only used that as a ruse to . . ."

He gave her another chilling smile.

Once again, she grabbed for the door handle and he thwarted her move. "Are you insane?" he demanded. "You could be crushed under the carriage wheels and killed, you know."

She gritted her teeth. "That would be one way of getting away from you!"

Still holding her with one hand, he reached into a bag beside him on the seat and took out several long cords. Before she was fully aware of his intentions, he had caught her wrists and was tying her hands together.

"You . . . you . . ." She could think of no name bad enough to call him. "Devil!" she shrieked. And then she began to scream at the top of her voice and kick him with all the strength she had.

It did not take him long to tie her trim ankles together, and then he pulled out a cloth, which he stuffed into her mouth, choking off the screams. "I would much rather this were a pleasant experience for both of us," he said, almost sorrowfully, "but if you insist on having it otherwise, I shall bow to your wishes." From a sitting position, he made her a mock bow.

She made a guttural noise in her throat, the most she was able to do through the gag.

"The gag will stay in place until you decide

to stop trying to alarm the populace. When we are out of the city, I will remove it."

She struggled for a minute but quickly saw the futility of her efforts. When she tried to move her hands or legs, the cords cut into her flesh like dull knives, and the discomfort of the gag was unendurable. She tried imploring Gower with her eyes. He did not take his eyes off her, but his look had nothing of friendliness or sympathy about it. Finally, when she could stand the sight of his face no longer, she lowered her eyes and stared at the floor of the carriage. She had once thought Gower boyishly appealing, with his tousled blond hair and twinkling blue eyes. But now he was neither boyish nor appealing. There was a grim look in his eyes that said clearly that nothing and no one would stop him from doing whatever it was he wanted to do.

For a fraction of a second, she thought of the coachman as a means of help, then discarded the thought. He was in Gower's employ, of course, otherwise he would have stopped the carriage when she had started screaming.

When she looked out the window again they were out of the city, riding through the countryside. She made a noise in her throat to remind him to remove the gag. He gave her another of his infuriating smiles and obliged.

"There now," he said. "Is that better?"

"You insufferable cad! You unconscionable

scoundrel!" she spat. "I'll see that you spend the rest of your life in Newgate for this!"

He held the cloth up before her warningly. "Unless you want me to use this again, you had better be very careful of what you say and how you say it. I'm beginning to like you much better when you are quiet anyway."

Her mouth was open to utter a few more choice epithets, but she closed it firmly, silently vowing that she would say not another word to him. She would merely wait and watch for her chance to get away.

It seemed that the ride would never come to an end. On and on they went, through one small village after another, down long country roads and winding paths through forest land. Just as it was turning from dusk to dark, she saw what appeared to be several lanterns by the side of the road. The carriage turned and she saw a large building of stone and half-timbers just off the highway. The lanterns lit the front of it and its name was lettered on a large board nailed to a tree: The Jolly Junction.

Gower gave a sudden laugh. "Appropriate, isn't it?"

She did not answer.

"The Jolly Junction," he said. "Junction means joining, a union, you know."

Still she said nothing, but her face amply expressed the repulsion she felt.

"Sorry, dear heart, but I can't take any chances." He put the cloth in her mouth again and tied another over it. "We have reached our destination."

The coachman opened the door and Gower got out, then reached in and pulled Zandra out, throwing her over his shoulder as though she were a sack of potatoes. He walked to the rear of the building, then up a flight of long, steep steps. The door he opened led into a long corridor with rooms on either side. He opened the first door on the left, went inside and closed the door before putting her down on a bed. It was a fairly large bedchamber with crudely made wooden furniture: a clothespress, two hard chairs without cushions, a small table and the bed.

"I will take the gag out and untie you and send a maid to make you more comfortable," he said, "but you must give me your word that you will not cry out or try to get away."

She nodded. She would have promised him anything to get that terrible rag out of her mouth.

After he had untied her, he left the room. She stood up, wobbly on her feet, and teetered to the door. It was locked, of course. Obviously, he had not expected her to keep the promise.

She went to the one window in the room and looked down. From the light of a lantern in the side yard, she could see a rocky slope about twenty feet below, but no means of escape.

She went back to the door and opened her mouth to begin screaming when it opened suddenly and a large woman, dressed in black with a white apron, came in.

"I wouldn't do that, dearie," she said. "I got my orders to knock you about some if you look like you're going to misbehave."

Zandra closed her mouth. The woman was taller than she by a good three inches and three times as broad. Her face, slightly pockmarked, was as hard as a keg of nails. "I'm here to freshen you up before your mister comes back."

"He's not my mister." Zandra spat the words out. "He is a common criminal who kidnapped me!"

"Kidnapped, you say." The woman laughed. "Well, I'd say there's a man who knows what he wants and how to get it." There was admiration in her voice.

"Look, my husband is the Duke of Melford, and if you will help me get away from this maniac, he will reward you well."

The woman's laugh was as harsh as her face. "I've already been rewarded well. Now, here is the basin if you want to wash up, and the chamber pot is under the bed. I guess the mister will bring your supper himself since he told me not to bother."

Gower returned before the woman left. He

nodded to her, indicating that she was to go. As she opened the door, Zandra bolted across the room toward it, only to be tripped by Gower. She fell to the floor so hard that all the breath was knocked out of her. The woman stood in the door laughing for a minute, then she was gone.

Gower helped Zandra to her feet, then pushed her down on the bed and tied her up again while she was still panting for breath. "For that, my little tiger, you get no supper," he said. "And you also will be deprived of my company for the rest of the evening. When you learn to behave better, you will be treated better."

He put the gag back in her mouth.

"No, please no," she tried to say, but the words came out as a mumble through the gag.

"It will have to stay in place for a while," he said, "because I do not wish you to disturb the sleep of others."

Without another word, he left her alone in the room.

It was the longest night of her life. She struggled intermittently, trying to loosen the cords that bound her, but only succeeded in rubbing raw, red sores on her wrists and ankles. The gag was the most uncomfortable of all, but with her hands tied behind her, there was no way to reach it. Finally, she stopped struggling and tried to rest. If she were to get a chance to escape tomorrow, she would need all her strength.

There was no doubt that the innkeeper as well as the maid had been paid by Gower to see that she did not get away. How many others were in on the nefarious scheme she had no way of knowing. Nor did she have the faintest idea why Gower would do such a thing. He could not keep her locked up for the rest of her life, and surely he did not hate her enough to murder her. Where was the advantage in holding her prisoner . . . unless he wanted to worry Jason. Could Gower hate Jason with so much passion? Not only passion, she decided, but insanity. Dear God, who would ever have thought Gower could be so cruelly jealous, so insanely vindictive?

However, that thought gave her some comfort. If worrying Jason was Gower's reason, it meant that Jason was all right, not lying somewhere injured and near death. She would have to hold to that thought, for it was the only reassurance she had. If she believed, as Gower had told her, that her husband was hurt or ill and near death, it would undo her. She knew that she could not survive long without him, nor would she want to.

It was impossible to sleep, so she tried to ease her mental anguish by thinking about Jason, remembering his dark hair, the intense dark eyes that were capable of seeing right through her; remembering the feel of his strong arms binding her to him in the act of love and holding her gently afterward; remembering the sound of his voice, deep and resonant in conversation with others, soft and loving when they were alone together.

If only, with all this remembering, she could conjure him up before her! If only he would find out where she was, come and smash the door down and free her.

There was only the shadow of a doubt left in her mind now about what had really happened. Jason was all right (she *had* to keep believing that!) and had not yet returned from France. Gower had merely used his absence to trick her into leaving with him.

The long, hideous night finally ended and bleak, gray light seeped through the window. Zandra waited for the sunlight to pour in until she realized that there would be no sun. A new thought struck terror to her soul: what would she do if it snowed? It had looked threatening for several days, and if it started now, it probably would be a deep, long-lasting snow. Even if she could manage to escape her captors, would she be able to find her way through snow? And in these clothes? She wore a French cambric gown and her thin house slippers, which she had not taken time to change before leaving with Gower. There was her pelisse, but it was not heavy enough to protect her in snow.

As she pondered this, she heard a key in the door. The knob turned slowly and Gower came in, smiling cheerfully.

"Good morning, dear Zandra. I trust you passed a middling good night." He stood beside the bed looking down at her. "I found out last night that I cannot depend upon your word, so I think it best to leave you bound and gagged."

She made a noise in her throat.

"Does that mean you will be a good girl and not call out if I remove the rag?"

She nodded vigorously.

He untied the knot at the back of her head and removed the long strip of cloth, then took the other from her mouth. She tried to speak, but her mouth was so dry she could only utter harsh, unintelligible sounds. She felt so weak and exhausted she knew she could not make enough noise to be heard outside the room.

Gower went to the pitcher on the table and poured her a glass of water, which he presented to her as though giving her diamonds. She swished the water around in her mouth, but swallowing was difficult. It took several tries before she managed to get it down her throat.

"You must swear that you will not try to leave this room or make any noise," Gower said, "or I shall tie you right up again."

She nodded.

"That's not good enough," he said. "I want to hear you say the words."

"I swear." Her voice sounded strange to her.

"You swear what? Say it all."

"I swear I will not try to leave this room or make any noise." It hurt to talk.

He rewarded her with a smile.

"How long do you plan to keep me here?" she asked.

"As long as necessary," he said, going toward the door. "I will send the maid now. She will see to a bath and breakfast for you. And if you try anything with her . . ."

"I haven't the strength," she said, realizing as she said it that it was true. She doubted she could even walk across the room without either falling or staggering like a drunkard.

The same woman who had come in the night before returned as soon as Gower went out. She had a tray of food in her hands which would have been welcome had not Zandra's mouth and throat still felt so peculiar from the gag.

"Pass a passable night, dearie?" the woman said, laughing as though she had made a joke. "Brought you some breakfast. Soon's you eat I'll bring water for your bath. Your mister said he'd bring your clothes when he comes back."

"He's not my mister!" Zandra found enough strength to speak. "I told you I am married to the Duke of Melford and that man you call my mister is a criminal." Where a bribe had not worked with the woman last night, perhaps a threat would today. "You are an accomplice to his crime, and you will be sent to Newgate along with him."

"Cor! dearie, wouldn't I just like that though!" The woman beamed. "There's a man I'd follow to hell and back, given the chance."

"You may have to," Zandra said grimly, realizing that nothing was going to work, neither bribes nor threats, sweet talk nor menacing words.

Ravenously hungry, she sat down to breakfast and by eating very slowly, she managed without too much pain to finish a bowl of porridge, some hot buttered bread and four cups of tea.

After the bath, she felt better, but still weak and tired from lack of sleep. She lay down on the bed.

The woman picked up the cords and reached for Zandra's hands.

"No, please don't," she begged. "I am not going anywhere. How can I with the door locked?"

The woman looked dubious for a moment, then put the cords down and picked up the gag.

"No, don't!" Zandra begged again. "I swore to Gower I would make no noise."

"Gower, is it? You know him pretty good, I'd say." She put the rag on the table. "If you make one peep, I'll come in here and knock the sense right out of your head. I'll be right outside."

Zandra closed her eyes, pretending to fall asleep as the woman left; however, in only a matter of seconds she lost consciousness, having had no sleep the night before. When the maid returned at midday with another tray of food, she did not even rouse at the noise of the tray being set upon the table.

When she did awaken at nightfall, Gower was standing at the window looking out. He turned when he heard her stirring. "Well, I thought you were going to sleep the night away as well as the day."

She blinked uncomprehendingly, and several minutes passed before she remembered her plight. "What day is this?" she asked finally.

"The day after you decided to leave your husband and run away with me," he said.

She was out of bed instantly, lunging at him, but she faltered after only one step. He caught her in his arms, holding her close to him.

"Let me go, you *criminal!*" She still was at a loss for a name bad enough to call him.

He helped her to one of the chairs, then released her. "See." He pointed to the table where the evening meal was laid out, complete with candlelight. "I am trying very hard to please you."

"The only way you can please me is to take me back to London this very minute."

"I am afraid that is impossible." He nodded toward the window. "It has been snowing for some time. It appears that we are marooned here." He began to chuckle deep in his throat. "And I can't think of a nicer way to spend a few days, can you?"

"I would rather be in a pit of vipers," she said as he sat down opposite her at the table.

"Let's have no talk of snakes," he said good-naturedly. "It was a snake that ruined the idyll of the garden of Eden. I prefer to keep our Eden perfect."

"*You* are the snake," she began, then stopped. Name-calling would get her no-where, and there were questions she wanted answered. "Gower, why did you bring me here? What are you up to?"

Very methodically, he took the covers from the dishes on the table and filled her plate. "What a lovely meal Blanche has brought us," he said.

"Blanche . . . is that the name of that harridan who guards me like a jailer?" she asked.

"Blanche Durban," he said. "Thoroughly reliable in every way."

"I am sure. But you did not answer my questions."

"This is quite a snowstorm outside. I am afraid it may last for days and days." He gave her a friendly smile. "As charming as you are, Zandra, it is necessary for me to tear myself away from you every few days and get back to London. I have to keep up with what is going on with the Queen and how long it will be before James lands on these shores."

"Is he coming?" she asked, interested at once. "Is Jason back, and did he bring the Pretender with him?"

He wagged his finger at her. "Now, now, I can't tell you everything, can I? Then you would know as much as I and have me at a disadvantage."

"You were at a disadvantage the day you were born," she mumbled. Then, louder, "Please, Gower, tell me why I am here and how long you plan to keep me here."

He buttered a piece of bread with infuriating slowness. "Can you not remember what very good friends we were?" he asked. "I can remember not so long ago that there were even thoughts of marriage . . ." He broke off, adding, "Everything is going to be all right between us again, Zandra. We will be just as we were before that fool duke came on the scene."

"Everything is *not* all right and never *will* be between us." She raised her voice. "Jason is my *husband* and I love him very much.

Can't you get that through your head, you maniac?"

"When Jason finds you have run away with me—after he reads the note I left him—he will be getting a second divorce." He laughed as though this struck him as quite funny.

"Jason will find me and he will kill you before you even have time to beg for your life," she said. "You may laugh now, but soon it will be a matter for crying."

"I am not laughing alone," he said. "All of London is laughing at Jason now because his wife has left him a second time and run off with another man."

She got up from the table, the sight of Gower and the food making her feel ill. Only one good thing had come of trying to make conversation with him: she knew now for sure that Jason was safe, that Gower had lied about the boat having sunk. But the rest of Gower's revelation to her made her want to burst into tears. Not knowing that Gower had forced her to leave, Jason would have only Gower's lying note to go by. How Jason would hate her as soon as he read that note! Why, the note probably would even preclude his making any effort to find her. By the time Gower let her go . . .

Her eyes narrowed as she turned and looked at him. She knew now what he was planning. He would keep her prisoner until Jason divorced her. By the time Jason had gone through a second divorce and all the unpleasantness that went with it, he would hate her. The damage would have been done and there would be no way she could ever make it up to him, or even make him believe that she had not gone willingly with Gower.

"You are *vile*," she said, her words cutting through the room with the sharpness of a knife. "You are no better than a stinking dung-heap, and I wish I never had to see your face again."

The smile finally left Gower's face. Scowling, he arose from the table, crossed the room to her in three steps, and caught her by the arm, his fingers pinching her flesh. "I had thought we would have a nice evening together," he said, "but I see you are in no mood for conviviality. You need more time to think."

"All the time in the world would not make me think any better of you," she declared.

He picked her up and threw her upon the bed, reaching quickly for the cords that lay on the floor. "We'll see about that," he said as he began to bind her wrists.

She struggled against him. "No, don't!" She opened her mouth to scream, but he clapped his hand over it. "It's your own fault that you are going to spend another night trussed up like a pig on a spit. I had other more enjoyable plans for you."

He put the gag in her mouth as he talked, and then he tied her ankles. When he finished, he gave her one disgusted look and stalked out of the room, slamming the door behind him.

Chapter Eighteen

GOWER HAD REACHED THE LIMIT OF HIS
patience—and gone beyond. He had waited for
Zandra's animosity toward him to mellow for
far longer than he had ever waited for anything, probably because he wanted her more
than he had ever wanted anything else in his
life. But he wanted her to want him also. He
had no interest in taking any woman by
force, least of all Zandra. For that matter, he
wasn't even sure that he *could* take her by
force.

Snowbound at the inn for the past three
days, he had stayed out of Zandra's room,
leaving her to the not-so-tender ministrations
of Blanche. He hoped that when he decided to
visit her again, she would have become so

sick of that bull of a woman that she would welcome him as he wished to be welcomed.

Meanwhile, the inactivity and the boredom were about to turn him into the maniac she had called him. He had spent most of the past three days in the public room of The Jolly Junction drinking ale and talking with the other snowbound wayfarers, not one of whom interested him in the slightest.

On the fourth day, an idea struck him that was so ingenious that his spirits rose at once. He had thought he would send his coachman back to London to get Zandra's clothes from the house on Mount Street. That was to be the final part of his plan, the real *coup* that would make Mrs. Wallace and the duke understand that Zandra was with him willingly and wantonly. The snowstorm, however, had ruined that scheme. It was on the day after the snow stopped that it occurred to him that the way to Zandra's heart was to buy her an entirely new wardrobe, a sort of trousseau. And perhaps a jewel or two. There was not a woman on earth who could resist the latest fashions and a few expensive baubles—and if he were any judge, it had been many a year since Zandra's gowns had been in the latest fashion.

The afternoon shadows were lengthening across the snow and Zandra watched them from the window, imagining that the shadows took the forms of lurking animals. If she did not get out of this room soon, she would become as daft as Gower. Sometimes she slept during the day and awoke not knowing what day it was or exactly how long she had been locked up in the room.

Today she was near famished, for she had had no food brought to her since breakfast. Was Gower going to try to starve her to death?

It's about time, she thought when she finally heard the key in the door. She turned and saw Gower entering, his arms loaded with boxes. She had wondered where he was during the past three days, but she would not have inquired of Blanche for anything on earth—except her freedom.

He smiled broadly at her as he put his packages on the bed, the table not being large enough to hold them all. Zandra smiled back, not because she was glad to see him, but because she had noticed that with his arms full, he had not locked the door behind him.

She could tell that her response had pleased him; his face was absolutely radiant now.

"Come see what I have brought you," he said.

She edged slowly to the side of the table nearest the door. "You show me," she said.

"Happy to." He hummed a little tune as he opened the first box and took out a sprigged muslin and a silver and green satin.

"Lovely," she said. "And how do you know that they will fit?"

"Blanche said they would."

"To what festive occasions shall I wear them?"

"Right now you can wear them here, for me. Later, you can wear them to the social occasions we attend."

"I see." A few inches more as he opened a second box that held two more gowns, a dove gray traveling suit and an apple green promenade gown.

"There's another gown in that box," he pointed, "and some other things you may need. You can open them later. I want to show you this." He took a small box from his coat and opened it.

It was her only chance. She bolted for the door and was turning the knob before he caught her and half pulled, half carried her back across the room.

"Zandra, don't be that way," he said pleadingly. "Can't you see how much I love you, how much I want you?" He pressed her to him in a suffocating embrace. "Just see what I have for you." He watched her warily as he picked up the box from the jeweler's, took out the brooch and the earrings and put them in her hand.

She gave them one quick look and threw them in his face.

"Damn you for a vixen!" he cried. "I was trying to be nice to you, to beguile you with kindness and loving words, but you are not worth the effort." His arms tight around her, he tried to crush her mouth beneath his, but she fought him, twisting her head away and beating on his chest with her fists.

"Get out of here and leave me alone," she gasped.

"I am going to spend the night in this room," he said. "I have waited long enough."

She managed to twist out of his arms and again flew toward the door, but he caught her by the arm.

"Are you going to behave yourself . . . as a woman should?" he asked, and for answer she bit his hand.

"All right," he said between clenched teeth, "you shall get as good as you give." He picked her up and threw her down on the bed and before she could move he was half pulling, half tearing her clothes off. She had never seen him so angry or frustrated. It had not occurred to her before that Gower was a physical threat, but now she was terrified! She opened her mouth and let out one piercing scream after another, and when he put his hand over her mouth to stop her, she bit his finger until he howled.

Suddenly the door was flung open and a big, black-haired man filled the doorway.

"What do you want?" Gower roared. "Leave us be."

His eyes bright with lust, the innkeeper said, "If you can't keep your woman from screaming like that you'll hafta take her somewhere else." Even when talking to Gower, his eyes never left Zandra.

"Help me!" Zandra cried, trying to pull a quilt around her and get off the bed at the same time. "He has kidnapped me."

The innkeeper ignored her as completely as though she had spoken in a language he could not understand. "Can't have that yelling going on up here," he said to Gower. "Do something about it or take her somewhere else."

"Don't worry," Gower said, "you won't hear any more noise from this room. I'll go elsewhere myself until this wildcat becomes tamer."

The man stood at the door staring for another full minute, then backed out and shut the door.

Zandra began another scream only to have it choked off in the middle as Gower slapped her hard across the face.

"Why do you have to ruin everything?" he said disconsolately. "Tonight was to have been so beautiful, a night we would always remember."

"I will have no trouble remembering it,"

Zandra said, "and I will tell the judge minute by minute what happened."

Gower reached down beside the bed and got the cords and gag. She did not even resist as he began to tie her up for she knew it would do no good.

"I will tell you one thing," he said, finishing tying her wrists and beginning on her ankles, "I will never let you go until you let me make love to you."

"Then you will spend the rest of your life as a jailer," she said.

His face was flushed with anger as he stuffed the gag into her mouth, threw the quilt over her naked body and left her to another night of misery and sleeplessness.

Chapter Nineteen

For two weeks Jason lay on the brink of death. "He has no will to live," the doctor told Emma, "and when the will to live is gone, the chances of recovering from so serious an illness are almost nonexistent."

During the day Emma allowed the servants to spell her at Jason's bedside while she tried to rest, but at night, when Jason was more restless, she herself sat beside him. When he began calling out Zandra's name, as he did almost nightly, she would lean over and say distinctly, "She is coming back, Jason. She will be back very soon, and you must be well by then. Get well, Jason, so you can greet her at the door when she returns."

Somehow the words seemed to get through

to him; invariably he would stop tossing about and lie quietly for a while. She could only hope that the words she spoke were true, but with every day that passed her hope of ever seeing Zandra again, along with her hope for Jason's recovery, diminished. The thought had come into her mind that something terrible had happened to Zandra to prevent her coming back. She knew her niece well enough to be certain that if Gower had kidnapped her, as she suspected, Zandra would somehow get away from him . . . if she were physically able. Emma would never believe that Zandra had gone voluntarily with Gower, no matter what Samuel had seen.

One night during the third week of Jason's illness, Emma looked at him as she sat beside his bed and saw that his eyes were open and was almost sure that for once he was not delirious. She felt his forehead and it was warm and damp, but not feverishly hot. She brought the candle closer and looked at him.

"Emma?" he said weakly.

"Yes, Jason?"

"Is Zandra home yet?"

If only she could say yes! "She will be here soon, Jason, very soon."

"I hope so." With that, he turned over and seemed to sleep normally for the rest of the night. When the doctor came the next morning he declared that Jason's fever had broken and that, little by little, he would begin to improve.

"Thank God," Emma said. Then she went to bed herself and slept for ten hours, her first real rest since Jason was taken ill.

The following week Jason was so much improved that he was allowed to have visitors. The first to call was Lord Dysart who, though he had known how seriously ill Jason was, was totally unprepared for how ill he still looked.

"You gave us a scare, my friend," he said. "We are all thankful you are on the mend now."

Jason was sitting in a chair in his bedchamber. Tomorrow he was to go downstairs for the first time. Since his first question to Emma on returning to full consciousness, he had not mentioned Zandra's name, and had promptly changed the subject if Emma seemed about to mention her. There was no doubt in his mind now that she had run away with Gower and he did not want Lord Dysart to bring up the subject either. He liked the elderly man and wanted to keep his friendship, but he knew that would be possible only if neither of them ever referred to Lady Dysart's nephew. To prevent any such conversation, he said quickly, "What can you tell me about the Queen? Does she still live?"

"Not only does she live, she has returned to London, ill as she is, to give her support to the House of Hanover." His lordship shook his head as though he could not believe his own words.

"She is truly indestructible," Jason said. "She will outlive us all."

"I am told every day that her death is likely to occur before the sun sets, but she remains among us," Dysart said. "Perhaps the Lord wants all of these pesky issues of succession settled before He takes her."

Jason gave a weak laugh. "Possibly."

"I must go now or Mrs. Wallace will be up inviting me to leave. She told me to stay only a moment or two." He stood up. "I think you will be out and about before long if that one has anything to do with it."

"She has everything to do with it," Jason said. "I owe her my life." His vague memories of the long illness told him this was true though he could have given no specific reasons for saying so.

Within two more weeks he was walking about the house, much of his strength having returned. He had even been told by the doctor that he might venture outdoors when the weather turned warmer.

He was sitting by a window in the morning room one day, a book in his hands but his mind on Zandra as usual, when he saw a familiar figure get out of a carriage and enter the house next door. "Good God!" he murmured, leaping up instantly.

"What is it, Jason?" Emma was sitting on the other side of the room, working at her embroidery. "Where are you going?" she asked in alarm as he ran out of the room.

There was no answer. Jason was out the door and at the front door of the Dysart house before Emma had put aside her embroidery.

Clemment, his usually unruffled countenance showing evident distress, said, "Shall I tell Lord Dysart you are calling, Your Grace?"

"No," Jason breathed, "this is the one I want to see."

Gower, standing beside Clemment, paled. He did not have time to utter a word before Jason grabbed him by the neck, almost choking the breath out of him.

"Where is Zandra? Where is my wife?" Jason demanded.

Gower finally twisted out of Jason's weakened grasp and took a step backwards. "I have not a notion," he replied coolly. "She is not noted for staying long with the men she professes to love. She left me also . . . after only a fortnight."

Jason stared at him open-mouthed and Gower took advantage of the surprise on the other man's face to continue. "A very fickle woman, that." He added, chuckling, "But there is none better between the sheets."

Enraged, Jason raised his arm and planted his fist solidly in Gower's face and the sound of crunching bone was clearly audible in the entryway.

"Oh my!" Clemment gasped and ran to get Lord Dysart.

Gower fell to the floor moaning and holding both hands over his nose as though that would stop the profuse bleeding. Jason threw himself on top of him to finish the beating he had begun, but he was deterred by a loud scream. Looking up, he saw Lady Dysart in the doorway and her husband only a few steps behind her.

Lord Dysart helped Jason to his feet and then Gower. Then he returned his attention to Jason. "You must not waste your strength on Gower. He is not worth killing . . . and I am not entirely sure your wife is worth killing for."

"There, there," Lady Dysart murmured to her nephew. She had given him her lace handkerchief to try to stop the blood gushing from his nose.

"Gower, I believe we can do without your company here at this house in the future," Lord Dysart said sternly. No matter if the boy was his wife's nephew, he could not condone his running off with another man's wife. "Please do not come back."

Jason, still unsteady on his feet, turned and walked out. Though he wanted to pound the life out of Gower, he did not want to hear the chastisement Dysart was giving the reptile, for that would mean having to listen to talk about Zandra's leaving him. He did not want to hear Zandra's name or anything about her.

Zandra took off the sprigged muslin and put on a dressing gown even though it was hardly dark outside. She had taken to going to bed quite early as a means of escaping boredom. Sometimes it worked; other times she would lie in bed for hours, knowing that it could be dawn before she even felt an urge to yawn.

Sometimes she felt she might lose what was left of her mind. Once, she had been so desperate for human companionship that she had even tried to engage Blanche in conversation, but that crone, suspicious of an escape attempt, had beat a hasty retreat from the room as soon as she had left the food tray.

Zandra was no longer bound and gagged. It was not necessary, for she could not get out the locked door and she also knew that screaming would do no good. She had tried it once more, only to have the innkeeper come to the door and threaten to "bash yer head into the wall if yer don't stop."

She got into bed, wondering if this would be one of those nights she could sleep or if she would lie awake for hours. Though she tried to control her thoughts, sometimes it was impossible. For a while she had amused herself by imagining how it would be when she and Jason were together again. Then, as more and more time passed and Gower did not come back to the room, she began to wonder if she ever would be set free. And finally, she knew. It took a long time for the thought to reach the front of her mind, but when it did she wondered why she hadn't thought of it before. Gower was not going to return. She had let him know that she would never let him make love to her and, since that was his only interest in her, he had turned her over to the innkeeper and Blanche to do as they pleased with her. What they pleased was what kept her imagination busy. Would they sell her as a slave to some foreigner? Put her in a brothel? The dire possibilities were endless, and these were the thoughts that kept her awake.

She did not know how long she had been lying on the bed tonight, one hour, two, when she heard the key turn in the door. Blanche had long since brought her supper and then come back for the tray, so there was no reason for anyone to be entering the room now. She raised her head just enough to see the door opening slowly and then, silhouetted against the wall by the candlelight, the innkeeper stealthily came into the room. He closed the door behind him and blew out the candle. Quietly, Zandra slid out of bed on the side near the wall and crawled under it.

"I hear yer so I know yer awake," the gruff voice said.

She felt the bed shift under his weight as he sat down, apparently thinking she was still in it.

"Not here, huh? Well, yer can't hide from me, dearie." He lit the candle again, and she saw the light swaying around the room as he looked for her. Then the light was lowered to the floor and she saw his face clearly as he looked under the bed.

"Aha!" he yelled. "Now I got yer. Yer friend's money is about used up so yer'll havta start payin' yer own way now."

Half under the bed himself, he reached for her, but she kicked wildly, hitting him in the face with her heel. He grunted, cursed and withdrew temporarily. Next he tried to grab her from the foot of the bed but again she kicked at him, this time hitting his shoulder. Again and again he tried to reach her, but each time she retreated and kicked him with all the force she could muster. After about fifteen minutes, he began to realize that he was not going to get his captive that way. Cursing her again, he got up off the floor. She heard him walk to the door, open it and say, "Yer can't spend the rest of yer life under the bed, dearie, so I will have yer sooner or later, never yer fear."

When she was sure that he had gone and

was not just waiting in the hallway, she got out from under the bed. She spent the rest of the night sitting in a chair just in case he returned.

She was still sitting in the chair when Blanche arrived with her breakfast the next morning. Half nodding, she sprang up, fully expecting to see the innkeeper coming across the room. The woman gave her a disgusted look, set the tray on the table and went out without a word.

It was a long day. Zandra wanted to sleep, but she was afraid to close her eyes for fear the terrible man would sneak in and catch her. She kept herself awake by trying to think of some way to escape, not that she hadn't exhausted the two or three possibilities that had occurred to her already; like hiding behind the door when Blanche opened it and scooting out, or hitting Blanche over the head, or pretending to be asleep and then darting out. The trouble was Blanche was too wary, too cautious, always checking to see exactly where Zandra was before coming all the way into the room. But perhaps she could try . . .

The door was opening. It was too early for Blanche to be bringing her supper so it could only be . . . "Gower!" she exclaimed as he came into the room. She had never imagined that she would ever be glad to see him, but she was now. "Have you been in an accident?" His nose was heavily bandaged. An accident would account for his not having come for so long.

"You might call it that," he said, and smiled suddenly. Had he imagined it or was she actually happy that he was here? "My nose was broken about three weeks ago."

"How did it happen?" She was not really interested, for there were other things she needed to tell him, but if she could get him in a good mood by inquiring about his injury, it might work out to her advantage.

"I was hit in the face by . . . something heavy." He locked the door, then went over to her, took her hand and kissed the fingertips, then her wrist. "You are just a little glad to see me, are you not? If the degree of gladness is dependent on the length of my absence, I should have stayed away a little longer."

"Yes, and find me murdered." She pulled her hand from his. "The innkeeper came in here last night and tried to attack me. I managed to keep out of his reach by getting under the bed. He is too fat to get all the way under. But he threatened to come back. Please, Gower, for the love of God, let me go home!"

"Tried to attack you!" He looked at her as though he were not sure he believed her. "But I paid the man a fortune to let me have this room with no questions asked and Blanche to take care of you." Then, as the full impact of what she had said and the possibility of what might happen in the future hit him, his ire was mammoth. "Why, that bastard is going to regret the day he was born!" He bounded out of the room, slamming the door behind him. Zandra heard his retreating footsteps as he ran down the hallway.

There was no way he could have locked the door, for he had started running down the hall as soon as it closed. Zandra went to the door, tentatively touched the knob and then turned it. She pulled the door slowly, slowly forward and then looked out into the hall. There was no one in sight.

She went out into the hall, to the door leading to the outside steps. Holding her breath, she tried that knob, and it also turned freely. She stood for a minute at the top of the steep steps, and looked about to see if there was anyone around. Quickly, she dashed down the steps and began running toward the forest next to the inn. Watching her footing as she crossed the rocky ground, she was unaware of the massive figure that appeared suddenly around the corner of the building until it met her head-on. She screamed as Blanche's big arms encircled her. "Let me go!" She struggled furiously, even trying to bite the thick arm holding her. "Let me go!"

"Thought you'd be smart and get away, huh?" Blanche grunted, dragging Zandra back across the slope and up the steps. "We'll just see about that."

They arrived at the doorway of the hated room just as Gower came back down the hallway. "What . . ." he began.

"She tried to get away," Blanche said. "I was over by the well and saw her heading for the woods."

"Thank you," Gower said. "Now get out and shut the door behind you."

Blanche smiled as though relishing the punishment Gower would inflict upon Zandra, and then did as she was told.

An all-consuming terror was building up in Zandra as she began to consider what might happen now. "Please, Gower, let me go," she begged. "You can't be enjoying seeing me suffer like this and—"

"If you're suffering, it's your own fault," he told her absently, his mind on more pressing problems. He knew now that he could not leave her here to be raped by that surly dog who called himself an innkeeper. Also, the inn was too far from London for him to make the trip more than once a week, and with things coming to a head concerning the Queen and her successor, it was important that he remain in London.

"Pack your things," he told her suddenly. "I

am going to take you back to London with me where I can keep an eye on you." As another thought struck him, he added, "I think our alliance will develop far better when we are under the same roof constantly."

Chapter Twenty

Spring gave way to early summer, but except for the seasons little had changed as far as Jason was concerned. The Queen still clung to life by a thin thread; daily London predicted that the thread would break momentarily. The Jacobites had turned into rabble-rousers on behalf of the Pretender, meeting constantly to try to devise a way to get him back on English shores. The Electress Sophia of Hanover, whom Anne disliked intensely, had died, leaving her son, George, heir presumptive to the British throne. And Jason, though fully recovered physically, fought long bouts with depression, then fought even longer ones trying to cheer up Emma. It was hard to tell which of the two spent more time in abject misery.

Jason had no idea now what to think of Zandra's disappearance. Emma was, and had always been, of the opinion that Gower had forced Zandra to go away with him, and Jason wanted so much to believe it that, occasionally, he did. But Gower was seen almost daily in London now at one Jacobite meeting or another, and he was never in the company of a woman. Where was Zandra?

Emma was sure that Zandra was dead, which was the cause of her freely flowing tears, her constant depression. Over and over during the past months she had assured Jason that Zandra would never leave him voluntarily. Now he almost believed it. One thing he did know: Zandra never would simply stay away like this without letting her aunt know her whereabouts, or at least that she was safe.

Sometimes Jason sat in the library for hours, turning a brandy snifter round and round in his hands as he thought. There was never any conclusion to his pondering, for there was no way to make one and one add up to anything that made sense. When he had assembled the facts, thinking he had finally solved the problem, another fact would be dredged up in his memory that would throw the arrived-at conclusion into the realm of the ridiculous.

There was only one thing of which he was certain: that Gower knew more about

Zandra's whereabouts than he had told. Even assuming that she had left willingly with the cad and then had left him, he would have to have some idea, some guess, as to where she had gone.

By now Jason was not even sure he wanted her back, but for Emma's sake, if for no other reason, he had to find out where she was.

Finally he made up his mind to put his pride in his pocket and go to see Gower. Perhaps by being civil to the scoundrel instead of trying to kill him, he might get some information.

Telling Samuel to see that the carriage was brought around, he got ready for the visit.

Gower stood at the window of his Exeter Street rooms, his mind on the latest turn of events. Only last night he had heard the appalling news that the Queen had put a price of five thousand pounds on the head of her half brother, James Stuart. He had heard, months ago, that the Queen had said that she would never take that course, but obviously one or all of the members of her cabinet had succeeded in talking her into it. Sick, drunk woman! She probably had no mind left at all and could be talked into anything.

He sighed, turned away from the window and sat down in a large chair. He stared across the room at Zandra, her lovely face half hidden as she bent over a book, John

Dryden's play *All for Love,* which he had brought her yesterday when he returned from a meeting at the Bell-Weather Coffeehouse. He had found that by keeping her supplied with reading matter he could keep her reasonably content—now that she had found out that being in London did not make it easier for her to get away from him. Indeed, to escape from his rooms was even more impossible than to escape from the Jolly Junction had been.

So there had been very little problem with her. The only drawback was that there also had been no love with her. He had approached her time after time and she either fought him like a tigress or else began to shriek her head off and had to be gagged. He could, of course, just take her, tie her to the bed and have his way. But that was not really his way: he still wanted to win her love, to have her as a sweet, docile, loving mistress.

"What's the play about?" he asked, the silence beginning to weigh heavily upon him.

She looked up. "It's based on Shakespeare's *Antony and Cleopatra,* but Dryden concentrates on the period between the fatal battle of Actium and the suicide of Antony and Cleopatra. He doesn't stick too closely to historical facts—I think the plot is more from his imagination. An ingenious play, though."

Gower went back to the window. He was not interested in Shakespeare, Antony and Cleopatra, John Dryden or any other denizens of the past. His whole life right now revolved around two things: getting James Stuart on the throne and making love to Zandra.

He looked at her again. God, she was so desirable, so beautiful! He felt as though his blood were scalding his veins, so much did he want her. He walked over, gently took the book from her hands, bent down and kissed her cheek. "My lovely Zandra," he whispered.

She moved to the other side of the love seat, out of his reach. "I am not your lovely anything and never will be. How long, how long before that fact reaches your brain— assuming that you have one?"

Today was one of the days when patience was his ploy. He gave her a smile, returned the book and said, "How long, how long before you are willing to learn and appreciate what love is all about?"

"You have no conception of the meaning of the word," she snapped, opening the book again and ostensibly shutting him out of her fictional world.

He returned to the window. Instead of trifling with her now, he would do better to give some thought to the political pot that was about to boil over. If James could be slipped into—

His thoughts came to an abrupt halt. He had been looking absently down into the street at a carriage that had stopped below the window, and now he recognized the man who got out. "Good God!" he gasped. Quickly he crossed the room, jerked Zandra to her feet and dragged her into the bedchamber where she slept—and where he kept the cloths and cords.

"What are you *doing*?" she cried. "I wasn't making a sound." The gag stuffed into her mouth cut off further outcries as he busied himself with the cords.

"No, and you won't," he said. When he had finished, he crossed stealthily to the window in the other room, just as a knock sounded at the outside door. Gower almost stopped breathing. The knocking came again. Then, after three or four minutes of intermittent knocking, the noise stopped and Gower heard footsteps descending the stairs. He let out a long breath as he saw Jason get back in the carriage and drive away.

That had been too close. Suppose he had not seen Jason arriving and Zandra had started her infernal shrieking at the first knock? It made him break into a cold sweat just thinking about it. He could only hope that Jason would not return. But he could not count on it.

"Yardley!" he called, and his valet appeared from a back room. "I have to go out for a while. You may free the lady from her bonds as soon as I am out, but do not let her out of your sight. And if anyone comes here before I return, see that she doesn't make a sound."

"Yes, sir," Yardley said. He carefully locked the door after Lord Lawring's departure.

Jason looked back as he drove away from the building where Gower lived. For the second time, he was sure he saw Gower at the window. When he had first left his carriage to go in, he had seen the scum at the window, and now there he was again.

Jason drove slowly down the Strand trying to decide what to do next. Several blocks later, passing the Bell-Weather Coffeehouse, he pulled up. He got out and flipped a coin to a young boy, instructing him to keep his eye on the carriage until Jason returned. He walked quickly back to the coffeehouse and went inside.

"Jason!"

He smiled as he recognized the voice. "St. Trevan," he said, "do you spend all your time in this place?" He sat down at the table with his friend.

"Lately you could say so. We Jacobites die hard, you know. In fact, like the Queen, we don't die at all."

"You are wasting your time trying to bring the Pretender back," Jason told him. "It will never happen. I met him during the winter."

St. Trevan nodded. "I heard you went to

France for Bolingbroke. I also heard that you said you did not think James was suited for political prospects."

"I said that and more," Jason told him. He gestured toward the proprietor, requesting coffee. "He would not be a good ruler, my friend. He is weak, sickly even, and nothing on earth—not even hope of the throne—will make him renounce Rome."

"So we are to be stuck with George." St. Trevan shook his head. "No, I cannot accept that. Nor can the others of my persuasion. We are having a meeting here in just a few minutes to decide what to do next. When you first came in, I thought that was the reason you were here."

The mug of coffee was set down in front of Jason and he took a sip, made a face, then put it down. "No, I did not know about the meeting. I merely stopped in to learn the latest *on dits.*"

"I did not know you cared a fig for the social gossip."

"I don't, particularly," Jason admitted, "but after being out of circulation for so long, I keep having the feeling that I might have missed out on something."

"Yes, your illness went on for a long time. Are you well now?"

"Completely." He took another swallow of the foul-tasting brew. "One of these days I would like to find a coffeehouse that makes decent coffee."

St. Trevan laughed. "No coffee is as good as it smells. Too bad. But getting back to the news, I suppose you have heard that Anne has finally put a price on James's head. That is the reason for the meeting."

Jason did not answer. An idea had come to him suddenly. There was no doubt Gower would be at an important Jacobite meeting. Hastily excusing himself, he left the Bell-Weather and returned to his carriage, where he sat and waited. Soon he saw Gower approach and enter the coffeehouse. He immediately put the whip to his pair and started hell-for-leather back in the direction of Gower's residence.

He left the carriage on the Strand and walked around the corner to Exeter Street. It was twilight now and he could see a lamp flickering in the window where he had, only an hour ago, seen Gower. Obviously a servant was there or the lamp would not be burning.

Jason stood for a long time watching the window, but saw nothing. He still was not sure what he was going to do, but somehow he was going to get into that apartment. He had no specific idea what he was looking for and he tried to prepare himself for the disappointment of finding nothing meaningful.

Darkness came on quickly, making the lamp in the window look brighter. Taking a deep breath, Jason started toward the outside steps leading to the second story, then he stopped dead, staring. Thrown against the wall by the lamplight was a silhouette . . . a woman . . . Zandra! He would know that profile among a million others.

He took the steps two at a time and knocked loudly at the door. Would she answer? Or would she peer through the glass pane in the door first, recognize him, and . . . He knocked again, sure now that he heard movement within, but no one came to the door. The movement was more like a struggle, but there were no voices. After a minute or two the noise stopped. He knocked again, louder and longer. Then he heard a voice, a man's voice, call out, "Coming."

In another minute the door was opened by a youngish man, obviously a servant. Jason said the first thing that came to mind. "Lord Lawring has sent me to get the lady and take her to him."

The man looked at him as though he did not understand. "I beg your pardon, sir?"

"The lady in the next room," Jason said. "Lord Lawring requested me to fetch her. He is at a meeting and cannot get away and he said to tell you that I am to take the lady to him."

"Those were not my orders from his lordship when he left here."

There was no longer the slightest doubt in Jason's mind that Zandra was being held against her will. Had she not been, she herself would have come to the door during this discussion, for he purposely had been speaking extraordinarily loud.

"Situations change," Jason said. "Let me speak to the duchess."

"Duchess? There is no duchess here."

. "According to Lord Lawring there is."

Jason saw the flicker of fear and indecision in the man's eyes. "Either you let me in or I shall be back in three minutes flat with a constable and you will spend the rest of your life in Newgate as an accessory to kidnapping."

"But I . . . I . . ."

Jason's patience ran out. He pushed the door open, went in and landed a blow in the man's face. The man reeled backward and hit the wall, which kept him from hitting the floor. Then, with one terrified look at Jason, he ran out the door and down the steps.

Jason rushed into the small salon, looked around, then went through the entire apartment. He knew she was here; she had to be here somewhere. But she was not in either of the bedchambers or the other rooms. He looked in the clothespresses, wardrobes, even under the beds. She could not have vanished so completely. It was when he was looking to see if there was a back stairway that he found the servants' quarters, a small sitting room and an even smaller bedchamber on the other side of the kitchen. He heard movement in the bedchamber. Holding the lamp he had taken from the front room, he peered through the doorway, then rushed into the room, set the lamp upon a table and gathered the form on the bed into his arms. His heart was pounding and his eyes were misty as he took the gag from her mouth and began untying the cords that bound her.

"Zandra, Zandra," he said over and over, while she, crying brokenly, said nothing at all, just clung to him.

Chapter Twenty-one

GRAY CLOUDS ALMOST COMPLETELY OBSCURED the August sun and the crowd gathered outside Kensington Palace was quiet. There was an occasional whisper, such as "Do you think it will rain?" but other than that, not a sound. All eyes were turned toward one window in the palace, behind which the Queen lay dying. This time there was no mistaking her condition.

Late in July there had been an acrimonious meeting of the Privy Council at Kensington that the Queen had attended. Both sides had shouted insults at each other and had settled nothing. The effect of that meeting had brought the Queen to her deathbed.

Two days later the Privy Council had met again and during that meeting received word that the Queen was dying. The members of the council went at once to the Queen's bedside to ask her to confirm the Duke of Shrewsbury, a Hanoverian adherent, as Lord Treasurer. She hesitated only a short while as some inner struggle seemed to shake her, then did as she was asked, finally putting an end to the last of the Jacobite hopes, plots and plans. George of Hanover would succeed her. Though those about her knew, she did not seem to realize that this would be her last official act as Queen.

Jason and Zandra stood a bit apart from the others in that silent, waiting crowd, their arms about each other like young lovers. Even at this sad time they were still overcome with the joy of being together again.

"Poor thing," Zandra said quietly, "she cannot have had a happy life."

"I sometimes wonder," Jason said slowly, "if anyone born to royalty ever does."

"I would not change places with any of them," Zandra said. "I would not change places with *anyone*."

His arm around her waist tightened. Even after two weeks, he still could not believe his good fortune in having her back. As for Zandra, never had the world seemed so beautiful and she herself so free. The novelty of being able to go wherever she wanted whenever she wanted seemed as it would never wear off. And the joy, the sheer bliss of being

able to lie night after night in Jason's arms
. . . well, there were no words to describe it.

She would never forget the night he had
found her at Gower's. She had been reading
when the knock sounded at the door, and
before she could even close the book, Yardley
was behind her, his hand clasped over her
mouth. Then he dragged her back to his bedchamber, closed the door and gagged and tied
her. She could hear Jason talking to him and
she had struggled furiously, trying to make
enough noise for him to hear her. But her soft
slippers kicking against the foot of the bed
could not be heard outside the tiny room.

After a short time, she did not hear his voice
anymore and she assumed despairingly that
he had left, but then she heard someone walking around. She wondered why Yardley did
not come to untie her . . . unless Jason was
still there. She began rolling back and forth
across the bed and bumping the wall.

Then the door had opened . . . and there
was Jason . . . and everything in the world
was all right again. But she, who had hardly
shed a tear since the beginning of the terrible
ordeal, could not utter a word because of the
sobs that shook her whole body. She could
only say his name over and over in her mind:
Jason, Jason, Jason! And he also had been
moved beyond words.

Once he had freed her, they lost no time in
leaving the apartment and going home.

Samuel met them at the door, the dignified look on his face changing instantly into a full-fledged laugh. Before either Jason or Zandra could say a word, he called, "Mrs. Wallace, there is someone here to see you."

"Why don't you show them—" Emma began, coming into the hall. Then, seeing who was there, her hand flew to her breast, she gave a little cry, and promptly fainted. Jason caught her just in time.

Revived, she looked wonderingly up at Zandra. "Is it really you? I am not dreaming this?"

Zandra kissed her aunt. "If you are, so are we. Would you mind getting up and giving me a proper welcome?"

It was over claret that Zandra told them in detail what had happened to her. During the recital Jason's face reddened in fury and his fists kept clenching and unclenching, but he said nothing.

"I knew it was something like that," Emma declared. "I knew you would never go away with that snake. Dear Lord, Zandra, to think what you have been through! It is no wonder you have shadows under your eyes and are as thin as a skeleton."

"I am going to kill him." Jason spoke for the first time, and his emphatic words made Zandra shiver.

"No!" she cried at once. "You must not!"

"Not kill him after what he has done to

you—to me, to all of us!" He looked at her as though he thought her wits had gone begging. "Of course I am going to kill him—before the sun sets tomorrow."

"And then you will go to prison or to the gallows and we will be separated again." Tears were forming in Zandra's eyes.

"She is right, Jason," Emma said. "That scoundrel isn't worth giving up your life or freedom for. Let *him* be the one to go to prison. Have him prosecuted for what he has done."

"It would be my pleasure to kill him," Jason muttered.

"No, Jason," Zandra said quietly, "if you do anything at all to him—murder him *or* turn him over to the authorities—it will be against my express wishes."

He looked at her, a scowl shadowing his face and sparks of anger in his magnetic eyes. "May I make so bold as to ask why you want no harm to befall that villain? Have you formed an attachment? Is there more to this than you have told us?"

She laughed. "Calm down, my love. I am thinking of you and me, not Gower. If you kill him, we will be separated again, either by death or distance, and if you have him prosecuted, then the whole sordid story will be all over London. And who will believe that Gower kept me captive for so long without bedding me, either with or without my consent? I already have something of a reputation, you know. If it's all the same to you, I do not wish to make it worse."

There was a moment of silence, then Emma said, "She's right, Jason."

"You mean you prefer to let people believe that you went away with him of your own accord, and stayed away for months?" Jason asked, anger still in his voice.

"Does anyone know that I *was* with him?" she asked.

"Lord and Lady Dysart know that I suspected you were with him," Jason said. "No one else does."

"They certainly will not spread the word about their nephew," she said. "If anyone is tactless enough to ask questions, just tell them I was visiting my father near Beaconsfield. For that matter, I would like us—all of us—to visit Coulter Manor very soon."

Jason sighed. "All right. I will do as you wish concerning Gower, but I will never cease wanting to kill him. And as long as I live it will rankle that he hasn't gotten what he deserves."

"Thank you." Zandra leaned over and kissed him. "I think, sooner or later, everyone gets what he deserves, don't you?"

She stood up and suddenly swayed. She would have fallen had she not caught the side of a table to steady herself. The sheer nerve that had carried her through the terrible weeks of being locked up, of not knowing her future and being uncertain of her present, gave way and she found herself crying uncontrollably. Jason sprang to her side, holding her up while Emma also ran to her, not knowing exactly what to do. "What is it, lamb?" she crooned.

Unable to stop the tears, Zandra was becoming hysterical as Jason picked her up in his arms and strode purposefully out of the room, followed by the frightened Emma.

"What is wrong with her, Jason?" Emma asked as he took Zandra to their bedchamber.

"Her nerves have given way . . . finally," Jason said, laying her on the bed. "God knows how she managed to hold up this long."

Emma hovered over the bed. "Shall I call the doctor?"

"No," Jason replied. "She will be fine. I think all she needs now is to be quiet for awhile."

"Don't leave me, Jason," Zandra pleaded, almost incoherently. "Stay . . . with me."

He bent over her, stroking her hair like an anxious parent. "I'll be here, love. I won't leave you."

After Emma left the room, Jason undressed Zandra and wrapped her in her nightdress. Then he lay down beside her and took her in his arms, holding her close and murmuring,

"Hush now. Everything is all right. It's all over and we are together again."

Zandra clung tightly to him. After a while her breathing became deeper and he realized that she was asleep.

It seemed no less than astonishing to him that she could have withstood as much as she had. Only her amazing strength of character could have brought her through such a harrowing experience. Though not unscathed, the effects would lessen as the ordeal faded in her memory.

Getting up, he removed his clothing, and then lay back down beside her, taking her in his arms again. He needed to hold her close to him as much as she needed to be held.

It was a long time before he joined her in slumber.

She stirred first in the gray light of predawn and opened her eyes tentatively. The familiar surroundings were like a healing balm and the feel of Jason's arms around her brought tears to her eyes . . . but this time they were tears of happiness. "My dear, dear love," she whispered.

Jason awoke then, looking at her as though he could not quite believe his good fortune in having her back. Slowly his fingers traced the features of her face, and when he saw the love in her eyes, his mouth pressed down upon hers in a hungry kiss.

His hands stroked her body as if it were necessary for him to memorize again the feel of her soft flesh, and then his lips lovingly made their way from the hollow of her throat to her breast, while her hands caressed his long lean body, narrow hips and thighs. Each was breathless in the wonder of holding the other again.

His hands cupped her breast as his lips sought first one rosy peak and then the other, causing her to quiver with the searing sensation. She clung to him passionately as his lips trailed down her body, setting fire to the very core of her being. Then their bodies were molded together, his muscular hardness a contrast to her velvety softness. His lips were on hers again, possessively demanding entry while his leg pressed urgently against her thighs, separating them.

The slow sensuous rhythm of love quickly reached a fever pitch, their frenzied bodies straining toward culmination. Ripple after ripple of pleasure went through them both as his powerful movements took them nearer and nearer to ecstasy, ending finally in an explosion of sensation that brought gasps of rapture from them both.

They remained as they were, locked together in a passionate embrace, yet spent by the force of their fierce love-making. Their great need for each other had been satisfied, another hunger had been fed, but only temporarily. They made love yet again, being gentler and more leisurely this time.

"We must never spend another night apart," he murmured.

"I know," she replied. "I cannot live without you. I cannot *exist* without you."

Slowly, lazily, they matched each other kiss for kiss, caress for caress, until the embers burst into flames again. She delighted in the feel of his body pressed against hers, the faint tickling of his lips as they grazed almost casually across her shoulders. She tangled her fingers in his hair and half-smiled at him as her mouth parted in surrender. Then she moved against him languidly and he responded with a new surge of desire. He raised her hips to him, and once more they began the tantalizing climb to the peak of pleasure, higher, higher, into that rarified stratum where the sensation of feeling was all there was. Sharp, intense, exquisite, all-consuming . . . holding them hostage for a few glorious moments, then releasing them reluctantly. Afterward they fell into the deepest sleep either had had since they had last shared the same bed.

Now, looking up at the Queen's window, Zandra thought how sad it would be to have to leave this beautiful world, even with the hope of another, better world. She expressed this thought to Jason.

"Think of it this way," he said. "She has been ill for so very long, and soon she will be through with illness and at peace."

"And reunited with her prince consort," Zandra said.

A low murmuring swept through the crowd as a figure paused before the window, then moved on.

"Was that the Queen's physician?" someone asked.

"It was a woman, not Dr. Arbuthnot." The answer came from another small group.

Once again the crowd fell silent. For a few minutes, the sun came from behind the clouds and shone brightly over the homey palace. Large, utilitarian, completely without grandeur, the palace was very much like the monarch within: useful without being ostentatious, grand without being grandiose. Zandra felt a tug at her heart as she thought of the Queen and how ill she had looked at the supper at the Banqueting House, and how misunderstood that illness had been by so many of her subjects.

The clouds covered the sun once more, bringing temporary darkness to the palace grounds.

"Look, look!" came the whisper through the crowd.

Dr. Arbuthnot had come to the window. He took a white handkerchief from his pocket and slowly waved it to the crowd.

The Queen was dead.

Anne, the last of the Stuarts to rule, had died at age forty-nine. Before the day was over Jason and Zandra were told by Lord Dysart that her last words reportedly had been, "Oh, my brother! Oh, my poor brother!"

Epilogue

"Will Lucien be able to stay on the road?" Zandra asked Jason, looking worriedly at their carriage driver.

"If we were in the lead carriage, I should be a bit bothered," Jason said, "but, fortunately, we have others in front of us."

They and most of aristocratic London were on their way from the city to Greenwich to greet the new King of England. It was after nightfall and the fog swirled around them like dense clouds floating on earth instead of in the heavens. Even the lanterns hanging from the sides of many of the carriages were not of much help as the horses picked their way as slowly as plow horses on a rocky field.

Zandra, dressed in green velvet with a matching hat, gave a huge sigh. "I hope the circumstances of the King's arrival are not a sample of things to come."

"As do I," Jason said. "He certainly has taken his own good time in getting here."

It was the twenty-ninth of September, almost two months since the death of Anne, and the gossip mills had it that George was visiting half of Europe before traveling to England to begin his kingly duties. It was obvious, even to the most devout supporters of the House of Hanover, that the new ruler was able to keep his enthusiasm for his new country well within bounds.

"We can only hope for the best," Zandra said, and that was the attitude taken by all except the most rabid of Jacobites who still dreamed of bringing James Stuart back.

Because of the darkness and the fog, it was impossible to see more than a few inches away from the carriage. Therefore they were not aware that they had arrived at the Greenwich landing until the carriage stopped and Lucien jumped down to open the door for them.

"The King's barge is just up the river, I am told, sir," he said to Jason. "It is being rowed to Greenwich."

Jason laughed suddenly. "I must say his arrival is something less than regal." However, he changed his mind on looking around him. Others were alighting from the carriages, and in the bright light of innumerable torches, candles and lanterns was an array of silks and satins and velvets of every hue and design. The landing was a blaze of color as the nobility of London came out in all their finery, and in the background the beautiful buildings of Christopher Wren made a perfect setting for the King's reception. In spite of the fog, His Majesty could not help but be impressed by such a splendid turnout.

Since the wait threatened to be a fairly long one, Jason and Zandra got back into their carriage to escape the chill night air. Sitting in the darkness, they held hands like young lovers, perfectly content in a companionable silence.

Finally the cry went up, "Here it comes, here it comes!"

"They are referring to the King as an it," Zandra said, amazement in her voice.

"Not the King," Jason laughed, "the barge."

"I thought everything that floated on the sea was a she," Zandra said.

"Not necessarily, but—" Whatever else Jason was about to say was lost as a loud cheer went up, and then trumpeters were heralding the arrival of George of Hanover.

They left their carriage for the second time and made their way to the landing just as the barge docked and was being tied to the jetty. It still seemed an unseemly long time before the new monarch deigned to put his foot on English soil, and the titter of excitement grew fainter instead of louder as the minutes ticked away.

"If there were a Queen with him, he would be more prompt," a nearby woman muttered, and another voice said, "If there were a woman with him, it wouldn't be his Queen." His Queen, Sophia Dorothy, was still shut up in the Castle of Ahlden where she would remain until her death.

At that moment George appeared. First he looked from right to left, then he paused while an entourage of Hanoverian friends, advisers, servants and secretaries left the barge.

"He has brought his subjects with him, fearing he would find that all here have fled the country," chirped one wag in the crowd.

Then George himself stepped ashore, and his new subjects were confronted with a middle-aged, pale, little man with bulbous blue eyes and a long nose.

Once his feet were planted on terra firma he paused again as though waiting for accolades or some special ceremony to begin.

"Does he expect the coronation this instant?" Zandra asked.

The Dukes of Marlborough and Oxford stepped forth from the crowd to greet the new monarch and then they were followed by the old Archbishop of Canterbury. Zandra noticed that the King spoke to them in French.

Jason's tug at her elbow meant he was ready to do his civil and social duty. The two of them walked the few steps to where the little man stood. Jason bowed and Zandra dropped a deep curtsy as the Duke of Marlborough presented them.

"The Duke and Duchess of Melford."

George murmured something that Zandra recognized as German, but since she didn't speak the language, the King could have been telling her to go to the devil for all she knew. More likely, though, he was merely saying how-do-you-do or something equally inoffensive.

They stepped aside while a few others were presented to His Majesty. Each time he was addressed in English, he answered in German.

Finally it dawned upon Zandra. "Dear Lord!" she exclaimed, and not too softly, "the King of England cannot speak a word of English!"

She and Jason moved farther away while others of the nobility were presented to their new King. Either the fog was beginning to lift a bit or her eyes were becoming more accustomed to peering through the blur, for she was beginning to distinguish familiar faces among the crowd. It surprised her to see Lord and Lady Dysart, accompanied by Lady Lawring, near the edge of the crowd. She could not have said why she was surprised, because his lordship seemed to have given in with good grace, according to Jason, when he was told that James Stuart was unacceptable as a ruler. She also noticed, standing at the very back of the crowd, Jason's friend, St. Trevan. That was another surprise, for she had taken him to be an ardent Jacobite. Another case, she supposed, of giving in and making the best of things.

Suddenly, as her eyes continued to wander over the crowd, she gasped and cried, "Jason, look!"

Slowly making his way from the back of the mob, a pistol in his hand, was Gower.

Jason inhaled sharply, then pushed his way through the clusters of people to Gower.

Gower looked around and saw Jason advancing on him, but it was too late to get out of the way as Jason ducked, grabbed Gower around the knees and threw him to the ground. Gower squeezed the trigger of the pistol just as Jason reached for the gun, so the aim was off, but Gower's howl left no doubt as to where the bullet had gone. He got up and tried to run, but fell flat before he had taken a step. He had shot himself in the foot.

By this time the crowd had parted, giving wide berth to the two combatants, and polite conversation had turned to screams. Zandra pushed her way to the King's Guards, crying "He is here to kill the King; that man is trying to kill the King!" When the Guards continued to stand like statues watching Jason and Gower struggle, Zandra repeated the words in

ARDENT VOWS

French. It was George himself who translated the French to German for his Guards.

Like lightning, four of them pounced on Gower, shackled him and led him away as Jason got up from the ground—where he had already subdued the would-be assassin—dusted off his velvet breeches and white silk stockings, and returned to Zandra's side.

George approached them and grasped Jason's hand, thanking him in French for saving his life. "These Jacobites," he said, "they will never give up."

"They will have to, Your Majesty, in time," Jason replied, also in French. "There is no other course left for them."

The King shook his head. "No, they are stubborn and they will rebel again, but I shall prevail." A smile flickered across his pink face, then vanished. "I shall be pleased to see you and your lady in court," he said to Jason, then walked quickly to the royal coach waiting to lead the procession from Greenwich back to London.

In their carriage again, Zandra asked Jason, "Will Gower hang for what he did?"

"I doubt it. He is of the nobility and they seldom dance on the gibbet," Jason said. "But there is a good chance that he will become very familiar with the interior of Newgate."

"Do you think the King is right?" she asked. "Will the Jacobites rebel again? Or is this whole sorry mess over at last?"

"They probably will rebel again," he said, "but something about the way George said that he will prevail makes me believe that he will. Anyway," his arm slipped around her waist, "our part in it is over and now we can get on with our lives."

"I know something that will never be finished," she said. In the darkness he could not see the twinkle in her eyes, but he understood perfectly.

"I also," he said. And then he called to Lucien to leave the royal procession and hurry back home to Mount Street.

If you enjoyed the passion and adventure of this book...

then you're sure to enjoy the Tapestry Home Subscription Service℠!

You'll receive two new Tapestry™ romance novels each month, as soon as they are published, delivered right to your door.

Examine your books for 15 days, free...

Return the coupon below, and we'll send you two Tapestry romances to examine for 15 days, free. If you're as thrilled with your books as we think you will be, just pay the enclosed invoice. Then every month, you'll receive two intriguing Tapestry love stories—and you'll never pay any postage, handling, or packing costs. If not delighted, simply return the books and owe nothing. There is no minimum number of books to buy, and you may cancel at any time.

Return the coupon today . . . and soon you'll enjoy all the love, passion and adventure of times gone by!

HISTORICAL 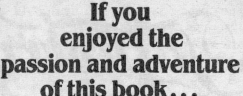 ROMANCES

Tapestry
HISTORICAL ROMANCES

Breathtaking New Tales

of love and adventure set against history's most exciting time and places. Featuring two novels by the finest authors in the field of romantic fiction—<u>every month</u>.

Next Month From Tapestry Romances

ALLIANCE OF LOVE
by Catherine Lyndell
JADE MOON
by Erica Mitchell

POCKET BOOKS